DANCE WITH ME

AN AFRICAN AMERICAN ROMANCE STANDALONE

A SWEETGUM MEADOWS ROMANCE
BOOK FOUR

IMANI PRICE

First Edition: August 2023

ISBN 978-1-960207-30-2 (ebook)
ISBN 978-1-960207-31-9 (paperback)

Published by Books to Hook Publishing, LLC.
www.BooksToHook.com

CONTENTS

CHAPTER ONE

With a ding and *ching*, their toast was finally ready.

Sean stood at the counter, dicing the onion until the chunks were minuscule. Tia loved the taste but loathed the texture. She had let him know the first time they had them.

"Uncle Sean, I can help, you know. Just show me what to do. Remember when I beat the egg that last time?" Tia twisted two strands of her hair. Her bed-head had left her hair messy. Every baby hair on her forehead stood in a puff, a result of her bonnet slipping away during the course of the night.

Sean checked the time on his phone next to the sink. Two water droplets left it blurry. "Still got time," he finished his dicing and lifted the cutting board, traveling to the stove.

Tia swung her legs under the table, finding the saltshaker a fun toy to play with. "Uncle Sean," she drew out, turning so she sat facing their stove by the fridge. She shook the saltshaker with her hand on its holes.

Everything was set: the onions, salt, white pepper, pre-blended seasoning, and eggs. Of course, the pan was on the stove with oil heating steadily. He heard his neighbor's engine rev through his over-sink window but did not take it as a sign to rush. "T, if you really want to help, you can go on and smear some butter on our toast, okay?" He cracked two eggs on the side of the pan. The yolks dropped beautifully into the oil, and its sizzle filled the air.

Sean listened to the clap of Tia's slippers as she hopped off her seat and bounced to the counter. The toaster was positioned toward the back of the counter. It was a bit of a reach for her small arm, but she managed to drag it closer to retrieve the toast.

"Be careful, T," Sean's arm whisked away, beating the eggs, counting the seconds as they passed. "As soon as you're done with that, you go get dressed, okay? I'll come do your hair when I'm done." He smiled while raising the white pepper.

"Ooo, can you do the poodle puffs with my hair today?" Tia handled the butter knife with ease. Despite tiptoeing, she made smooth streaks across their bread. She fit them neatly on the plate, too.

Sean sometimes wondered if her grace in the kitchen was in any way linked to her skill on the dance floor. Whatever it was, he appreciated it. The only reason he kept her from the kitchen most of the time was because of her age. Seven-year-olds around knives, fire, and heat were a recipe for disaster, at least in his opinion.

"I would, baby, but it's getting *pretty* late, so I'll just pull it all in one puff and add some gel to make it slick, okay?" The noises of life outside the window were growing; neighbors yelling exuberant greetings and the chime of bicycles.

Sweetgum's residents thrived in the rush of a Monday morning. The new week meant endless possibilities to this small town's people. There was nothing about Monday dread from what Sean had noticed. It could get overwhelming on days when he woke up on the wrong side of the bed, but for the most part, he embraced the optimistic air.

Tia brushed stray butter off her finger and onto her pajamas. "Okay," a tinge of disappointment came through her voice, but a second later, she dashed to the living room, doing a perfect in-air twirl before skipping to her bedroom. "Bet you can't finish making breakfast before I'm done showering!"

Sean laughed. "You wish!" He finished with the eggs and shut off the stove, ready to scrape the contents onto their plates.

THEY DROVE past his dance studio every morning on the way to Tia's elementary school.

He hummed along to the theme song of her favorite series playing through the car speakers. He drove past Rochelle's Old Fashioned Diner before turning onto the street that would take him to Sweetgum Elementary.

As he got lost in the melody, he glanced back at Tia in her seat, commending himself on the neatness of her hair. A sigh blew through his lips when he parked outside the building, taking in the happy elementary schoolers racing through the gate. The younger children depended on their mothers to hold their hands on the way.

Life's crazy, Sean thought when the engine shut off. He pushed open his door and stepped out, wondering what the nineteen-year-old Sean would have thought of this. *Raising a little girl on my own.* He'd never had a clear picture of what his life at twenty-nine would be, but it surely didn't include parenting a brilliant little girl who was sometimes too smart for her own good.

"All right, let's go," he walked Tia to the gate with his hand in hers, basking in the cool morning air and admiring the single cloud beside the sun.

"Good morning, Mr. Martin," greeted a mother as she leisurely walked through the gate, hand-in-hand with one of Tia's classmates. She fluttered her fingers and batted her eyelashes at him in greeting as she and the child followed the path to the school's veranda.

Sean gave a short but pleasant greeting in return, keenly aware of the curious gazes from the other mothers. One woman not only waved but winked, appearing content as she walked past the playground and reached the crowded doorway of pre-K. "Good morning to you, too," he answered hesitantly, slowing his steps.

Tia gently pulled him forward, a playful admonishment in her voice. "You're always like this, Uncle Sean. Don't act surprised. You know you're popular," she teased, stepping onto the veranda and releasing his hand, eager to join her classmates in the classroom. A cluster of little girls awaited her by the outdoor cubbies, instantly diving into animated conversations about the latest episodes of their beloved shows as soon as they reunited.

"What?" Sean chuckled affectionately, rolling his eyes fondly, and proceeded to follow Tia. He took her lunch bag and carefully slotted it into her designated cubby before departing.

SEAN DROVE BACK down Main Street for work. He parked his car near the town square, mentally reviewing his list of to-dos to prepare for the day ahead.

His fingers hooked in the top loop of his backpack, and he held it over his shoulder while walking to the building. It was a low-rise one-story structure with double glass doors as its entrance. Its square brick makeup didn't quite match the contemporary sign showcased there, but it would do. He liked the clash of old and new.

Lights, Camera, Dance! Sean read, taking a moment to marvel. His days as a dance student were filled with joy and contentment. Though he harbored a small hope of finding success as a backup dancer, his main aspiration was simply to lead a comfortable life. After graduating, he took the leap and established his own dance studio in his beloved hometown of Sweetgum. The initial months required patience and perseverance, but eventually, the studio gained momentum, and now things were flourishing. His proudest accomplishments included successfully paying off his business loans within the first two years of opening his studio.

He raised the window blinds upon entering the main studio.

Upon entering 'Lights, Camera, Dance!', students would encounter a front desk where classes were scheduled. The employee he'd hired to work there would arrive soon.

Sunlight poured onto the gleaming, waxed wooden floors through the expansive glass windows that adorned the back walls in a slender rectangle. From there, one could catch a glimpse of the street just beyond, where the local grocery store stood. Some more timid students opted to keep the blinds down during their lessons, seeking a sense of privacy. However, the majority of students felt at ease and didn't mind the outside world peeking in as they danced.

Turning away from the windows, Sean found himself face to face with his own reflection. The dance studio, like any well-equipped one, boasted a classic mirrored wall, offering an unobstructed view of his body. As he stood there, he couldn't help but notice how small he appeared in the expanse of the spacious, brightly lit room.

He met his own gaze in the mirror, reaching out to touch its smooth surface. Soon, the classes would begin. The first session of the day involved a delightful tango lesson with a group of spirited senior citizens. Every Monday, they gathered eagerly, often requesting specific dances to be taught for their next session. Sean cherished these moments, witnessing the older generation gracefully move their aging muscles. It was not only a joy to behold, but also beneficial for their well-being.

In the afternoon, Sean eagerly anticipated his ballet classes for children aged two to four years old. These tiny ballerinas were brimming with boundless energy, and he delighted in guiding them through their dance steps. Equally fulfilling was his class for children aged five to nine years old, the very class in which Tia participated. Despite her young age, his niece displayed remarkable talent in dance, and Sean couldn't help but take pride in the thought that she may have inherited some of his own dancing abilities.

"Once that's done, might grab a drink with Justin," Sean muttered to himself, beginning his stretching routine. With one elbow pointed towards the ceiling and his hand resting in the center of his back, he felt the tension release from his muscles. Justin, one of his best friends and the owner of Justin Time Clock and Watch Repair, would eagerly embrace the opportunity to hang out if his schedule allowed. Sean looked forward to the possibility of reconnecting later—it had been quite some time since they last hung out.

He exhaled onto the mirror, watching as his breath formed a transient fog. A sense of anticipation for the day ahead filled his heart. Sean knew that once they returned home, Tia might need assistance with her homework. He didn't want to disappoint her too frequently, so he made a mental note to research those "poodle-puffs" she had mentioned after she went to bed.

Sean's life revolved around dancing and Tia, which he considered to be of the utmost importance. Each day was a joyous adventure, yet there were moments while alone in bed when Sean's thoughts would wander. Was he content? Was this what he wanted? It was, but at the same time, there was a longing for more, a missing piece to complete his life's puzzle. It wasn't that Tia and dance weren't enough. No, he loved his niece and his work, but he had this yearning that was sometimes hard to shake. He shook his head, banishing the thought and replacing it with the familiar mantra: "Today is full of possibilities." He smiled, ready to embrace the day ahead.

The potent scent of coffee beans filled Nevaeh's nostrils, the warmth of her cup soothing her palms. With each customer entering and exiting through the door, her laughter bubbled forth, tickling her ribs and forming a symphony of mirth. What *was* this story?

"You did *not*," Nevaeh told Brandi, slamming her hand on the table. Nevaeh, Courtney, Brandi, and Joanne gathered in a booth near the front door. The cozy leather seats provided comfort as they sat across from one another, enjoying their drinks. Lunch at Joanne's was a regular affair for the four friends, but today held a sense of anticipation. Brandi had sent a text earlier, mentioning that she had an announcement to make, yet they hadn't yet delved into that topic.

"But I did. I really did, and it worked out well. The children *loved* him, and frankly, so did I." Brandi beamed over a successful performance she'd organized at the preschool. "Who knew he had it in him, right? He might have a future in stand-up comedy," she pressed her fingers against her lips to hide her giggles.

Nevaeh was not as contained. She howled on a laugh that made the story more humorous. Only after catching some patrons' stares, she followed Brandi's lead, suppressing her reaction.

Her friends were dying with laughter, though. No doubt at her embarrassment more than the joke. She joined them in stifled giggles as they lowered their voices. While fighting her tears which squeezed through her squinted eyes, she got this wholesome sense of appreciation. How lucky was she to have amazing friends that she'd known her whole life? Not even the passage of time or busy schedules could keep them apart. She loved these girls and hoped to know them forever.

Courtney finally caught her breath, using her hands to fan away lingering hysterics. "Guys, don't cause a scene. We're usually more well-behaved." She picked up her mug. "Okay, so that's Brandi; Nevaeh, what's new with you? Thought of a name for your event planning business? I've already got a couple of events in mind for you to organize," she teased, dancing with her shoulders.

Nevaeh fondly rolled her eyes as Joanne added to the *hilarious* question. "You know I haven't made any moves with that. Come on." It was her dream to open her own business like Joanne had done with Roasted Beans Coffee Spot, but for now, she was content putting her skills to use at the events committee in Sweetgum.

"And when will you? It's always the same answer with you, Nev. Acting like you don't have the skills to be the best party planner Sweetgum's ever seen," Joanne's tone seemed light, but Nevaeh knew that under the surface boiled frustration.

"Uh, I'll get there when I get there, okay? And I *have* been considering the steps I'd need to take to do that. But right now, there's just a whole lot with work and life and..." Nevaeh listed with her head shifting from side to side. She sipped her coffee, then rested the mug on the smooth wooden table, sweeping her silk-pressed hair off her shoulders as Brandi spoke up.

"I think that if you're serious about making a start, Joanne can help with navigating." Brandi's gentle approach contrasted with

Joanne's impatience. "And Joanne, don't push her; you know she doesn't like it," she scolded tenderly.

Joanne backed off with her hands up. She ran a fingernail through her freshly done braids, likely satisfying an itch. "I'm just saying. It's my way of encouragement," she sang, stretching the last syllable.

"Thank you, but I'll cross that bridge when I'm ready," Nevaeh mimicked her singing, prompting Joanne to sing back before Courtney put a stop to the back and forth. It was good that she did, too. Otherwise, things would have ended in a clashing duet.

Brandi smiled into her cup after sipping. "So, Joanne's doing great with this popping coffee shop, Courtney's art gallery is preparing for its grand opening, Nev's doing her thing at the planning committee, and I'm enjoying every moment with the children and parents," she had a glow to her as she blew a sigh of content. "You know I'm beginning to actually *like* Chelsea. Her ideas for playtime are getting better, and she—"

Nevaeh checked the time on her phone with a shake of her head. "Brandi!"

Brandi ceased her speech, raising her brows in surprise. "What is it, Nev?" she reclined in her seat with her cup to her chest.

"You called us here to discuss something important," Joanne reminded, her hands on the table. She cast an eye on the front desk every time more customers joined the already packed line.

Courtney gasped, "Oh yeah." Nevaeh wondered if she, too, had forgotten. They sometimes got lost in a realm of their own, catching up and laughing at fond memories and the happenings of their lives.

"What is it?"

Brandi face grew into a grin that lifted her cheeks. She sat straighter and sat her mug down. "Yes, my *amazing* news is that— well, first of all, you all know me and Chris got engaged recently and… oh, thank you," she paused for the soft applause and congratulations. "And, of course, with every engagement comes celebration."

Nevaeh found Brandi's happiness infectious. She was smiling like some kind of dope. "Aww. You're having an engagement party? Wait, didn't we have one already, or am I confusing this with something else?"

"This girl is *always* at a party. She can't even keep track," Joanne laughed. "I bet you were thinking about the last time we met up. *Everything* feels like a party when you're around,"

Nevaeh took the compliment bouncing her legs under their table. "Well, it's not like I'm trying, but thank you," she rested her palm on her chest, mock bashful.

"Wait, so you're really having an engagement party?" Courtney steered the conversation in the right direction. She seemed excited about what this might mean.

"Oh no. That's not where I was taking this. I was actually going to bring up the *bridal* party for my wedding." Brandi opened her arms to her friends. "Meaning all of you. Be my bridal party!"

The friends squealed like hyperactive fans at a concert. Courtney stole a tight hug while Joanne and Nevaeh clapped and sang, respectively. Nevaeh hummed the bridal march with a bump and a sway, adding beats where they weren't needed.

Brandi heard her rendition and danced along briefly. "Yes, I'd like all of you to be my bridesmaids, *with* the maid of honor being none other than…" she clasped her hands to her cheek while facing Nevaeh. "Our party planning princess," she chirped.

Nevaeh had been lost in her remix when the news was delivered. Her companions screamed again, this time with Joanne wrapping her arms tightly around Nevaeh's body. "Oh, my goodness!" It hit a second later, and tears sprung from her eyes. "Brandi!" she got up and ran around the booth to sit beside her friend, squeezing the life from Brandi as she tightened her embrace.

Brandi returned her affection but pushed her away. "I still have more to say," she said.

"I can't believe it! I'm your maid of honor!" Nevaeh exclaimed, overflowing with joy. The sheer excitement was evident on her face. They were all incredibly close friends, making it difficult to determine who would be chosen for such an important role. Did Nevaeh hold a special place in Brandi's heart, or was it merely a matter of chance? "I love you—"

"Yes, Nev, I love you too," Brandi chirped amidst the emotions. She cupped Nevaeh's face. "But there's actually a—are you listening, Nevy? Aww, I made her ugly cry," she held her yet again.

Nevaeh could hear Joanne's joyful excitement as Brandi brushed the back of Nevaeh's hair. She wished to have this moment for life. "Okay, sorry, sorry. Let me get it together real quick," she wiped her eyes and ended their second hug. Courtney and Joanne were staring like she was some puppy in a pet store. "I'm so happy, Brandi. I can't wait for—"

"Wup-pup-pup," Brandi cut her off right there, her finger raised. "There's a catch, and I'm just gonna say it before more distractions come up." She tapped Nevaeh's nose before starting. "You are going to have to star in a dance at my reception with everyone else during a dance circle we're planning. Yay! Dancing!"

The sentimental music in Nevaeh's head came to a screeching halt. "Huh?"

"Ooh," chorused Courtney and Joanne. They shared the same cringe. What was once a heart-warming moment turned awkward quickly. The silence would be deafening if Joanne's shop wasn't so busy. Conversations from surrounding booths floated to theirs, filling the uncomfortable quiet.

"Why would you do this to her? Can't she sit that out?" Joanne asked with her nose turned up. She seemed sorry for Nevaeh. "Unless you want a repeat of prom night where she broke Jacob's ankle," she cackled uncontrollably.

Courtney joined her in seconds, gasping for breath.

Nevaeh massaged her brow; her teeth clenched as her mouth stretched into a line. "I didn't *break* his ankle, but yeah, that was bad," she shook off the memory to address this new development. "Anyway, I don't think having me dance in this dance circle is a good idea. I mean, I have two left feet, remember? Remember Mrs. Brown nearly called an ambulance when I got down at Homecoming? Is any of this ringing a bell? She thought I was having a seizure!" Brandi knew these things, so this had to be a joke.

Of course, recounting such instances left Courtney and Joanne barking like seals. Their laughter once again drew attention.

Brandi hooked her arm in Nevaeh's as she tried to calm them. "Yes, I know she's not exactly gracefully gifted, but Chris and I really want this to be a thing. A nice circle where all the guests gather and, one by one, they come in and do a dance with their dates. You know, to get the vibes popping," she gently squeezed Nevaeh's arm.

Nevaeh rebuked this on all fronts. There were a few areas she was lacking, and dancing was one of them. It pained her to admit, but the truth was the truth. "Okay, yes, but I can't dance to save my life." She combed her hair with her fingers. "You *know* that. It's like my only flaw, Brands. Even perfect people have them," she joked. It was difficult to hear herself over Courtney and Joanne's laughter.

"It's not even just dancing. Nev, you are *clumsy*! Remember when she ran into the hall because of that roach and bumped right into a kid carrying pudding to the cafeteria? The mess was iconic!" Courtney brought up, her eyes glossy from laughter.

Nevaeh snorted at the memory, holding her head down as the ick of that pudding came back to mind. "Oh God, don't even talk about that," she covered her face with both hands.

"I'm still not over that time she *tried* to freestyle in the gym when Coach Matthew played those old hits. Like Nev, you *know* you can't dance. Why did you do that?" Joanne said, a smile splayed across her face. "I think you went down in history with that one. Be glad TikTok wasn't a thing back then 'cause you would've gone viral *easily*," she joined her friends as they laughed together, Nevaeh covering her embarrassment with more jokes.

Brandi's voice rose, reclaiming control over the table. "Yes, I understand all of that, but the maid of honor, in particular, has got to dance, all right?"

Nevaeh eventually yielded to appease her best friend. If the bride desired her to dance, she would have to comply, despite her own reservations about her dancing abilities. A sense of apprehension washed over her as she envisioned the potential disaster that awaited her on the dance floor. Admitting this insecurity was difficult for Nevaeh, but deep down, she was genuinely terrified. What if she stole the spotlight from Brandi and inadvertently ruined her reception?

After Joanne ran back to the counter and Courtney skipped out to take a call with Justin, Nevaeh slid her handbag over her shoulder. "All right, well, I should take off," she said to Brandi. Her friend had just stood to answer a message.

"Okay, but before you go," Brandi said, slipping her phone into her pocket and taking hold of Nevaeh's hand to provide comfort. "Listen, I know you're scared to participate in this dance, okay?"

Nevaeh was about to interject a denial, but Brandi raised her eyebrow in challenge. A wave of concern washed over Nevaeh as she nervously looked around for eavesdroppers. She dreaded the thought of this becoming known—her, the upbeat party girl, afraid of a simple dance? It seemed absurd and incredibly embarrassing.

"That's why I have another surprise for you." Brandi walked her to the door and pushed it open. The warm afternoon sun caressed their faces as they stepped outside. Nevaeh was quick to retrieve her sunglasses from the front pouch of her bag.

"What kind of surprise?" Nevaeh inquired, her eyes scanning the sidewalk for any prying eyes.

Brandi gleefully waved her hands near her cheeks, exclaiming, "Private dance lessons!"

Nevaeh was taken aback by the unexpected revelation, her arms instinctively crossing as a passing vehicle honked on the street.

"Dance lessons?" she repeated, her voice tinged with a hint of hurt. "Am I really that terrible of a dancer to you?"

"Oh no, no, I'm not trying to offend you at all," Brandi hurried to placate. "Although," she winced. "Between you and me…"

Nevaeh huffed, pushing her hair away from her forehead as a gentle breeze cooled her skin. "Okay, fine, I admit I'm pretty awful," she conceded, scratching the back of her neck beneath her wind-blown hair.

Brandi's gaze softened as she spoke earnestly, "Listen, I genuinely want the maid of honor to be involved in this, and I truly want you to take on that role. I knew you struggled with dancing, so I went ahead and booked you some lessons. I believe it could be beneficial in the long run—to help you overcome your fear and conquer something that makes you feel small." Brandi leaned closer, her head slightly lowered, trying to meet Nevaeh's eyes.

Nevaeh raised her face and sighed, straightening the front of her ruffled blouse. "Okay, fine, but I'll do it for you and you alone, okay? Just so I don't cause a scene at your wedding," she finally relented, a spark of anticipation flickering within her as she prepared to tackle this challenge.

"Yay!" Brandi exclaimed, enveloping Nevaeh in yet another hug, the third one that afternoon. "You'll do great, I promise. The dance instructor I booked for you is absolutely incredible. He has an extensive background in dance." Brandi retrieved a card from her pocket and handed it to Nevaeh. "You remember Sean, Justin's friend? He runs his own dance studio."

"Well," she said, slipping the card into her pocket. "I guess I'll give it a shot. No way to get out of it now, right?"

Brandi smiled, her eyes twinkling in the sunlight. "That's the spirit! I'm so proud of you, Nevaeh, and I know you'll make me proud at the wedding, too!"

Nevaeh smiled back, feeling a newfound sense of confidence in her abilities. She might not be the best dancer, but she had the determination and willpower to do her best and make Brandi proud. She took a deep breath and squared her shoulders before turning away to leave.

"Thanks, Brandi. I won't let you down," she said, her voice resolute. With newfound purpose, she made her way to the dance studio, determined to prove her worth and let nothing stop her from becoming the best dancer she could be.

CHAPTER THREE

"Okay, and remember to lift your arm that way—no, not like that, not like that," Sean instructed his 5:00 p.m. class, his back arched and eyes focused on the mirrors. This particular class consisted of a few moms from Tia's school who had requested special lessons for the month.

The woman who had been struggling with her technique wore a playful grin as she remarked, "Well, come and show us then. We need your guidance." Her forehead glistened with beads of sweat under the bright studio lights. They had booked an hour with Sean during school pickup the previous day, taking advantage of the gap between Tia's class and his private student at six. The hour was swiftly coming to an end, and so was the daylight. Despite the sun only being halfway through its descent, Sean turned around to turn on the studio lights in preparation.

He smiled sheepishly at the chortles and wolf whistles that followed. "All right, I think that's enough for the day," he declared, turning to face his three students. Sean applauded their efforts, and each of them returned the gesture with a bow. Despite the laughter, he could see the sweat streaks on their tank tops and leggings, evidence of the exertion they had put in. Regardless of their initial motives, they had managed to push their bodies and express themselves through dance. For that, he wanted to commend them.

"Great job, everyone. Shall we meet again next week at the same time?" They had requested guidance for a contemporary piece featured in a popular music video, and Sean had taken the time to familiarize himself with the material the previous night.

The women nodded, their breaths strained from the workout. "As long as you keep those pants on, we'll be there," one of them remarked, giving a thumbs up. They giggled among themselves as they turned away.

Sean felt a warmth spread across his cheeks as he watched them gather their belongings. He knew the type, the students who booked lessons hoping for closer interactions with him. If he had a dime for every one of them, he'd have quite the savings. Perhaps enough to buy Tia that new doll she wanted.

Sean said goodbye to the moms near the front desk, then heaved a heavy sigh.

"Humph," said Cynthia, setting her magazine next to her computer. She twisted herself to look through the door. "Got any hot dates out of that?" she snickered, tapping her mouse to open a window on her screen.

Sean stretched his collar to his forehead, dabbing the sweat from his face. "No, not really." He re-tucked his waistcoat into his ballroom pants. "Tia's in the office?" he asked, heading towards the end of the hallway. As he passed the practice room, he felt a wave of humidity hit his face and instinctively waved his hand to fend it off before making his way to his office. "Hey."

Tia sat behind his desk, sporting a paper crown on top of her head. "Hey," she greeted, swaying back and forth on the rolling chair as she scribbled in her notebook. The desk appeared oversized for her small frame, with folders and application forms towering around her.

"Be careful there, T. I wouldn't want you to fall," Sean cautioned, brushing a knuckle against his eyebrow to ward off more sweat.

Pausing her movements, Tia set down her pen. "Are you finished, Uncle Sean? I heard those ladies calling you 'fine,'" she grinned mischievously.

Sean playfully rolled his eyes. "They were just having fun, but let's not repeat what they said." He approached her side and peered at her work. "Ah, math. Looks like you're giving those problems a run for their money," he pointed to the tick marks indicating correct answers in her classroom exercise.

"Well… Ms. Francis did say I'm smart," Tia responded, swiftly writing across the page and effortlessly forming her numbers.

"And that's because you are. You're *very* intelligent," he patted her head. "Keep doing what you're doing, okay? I've got one more class to take care of," he jogged through the door and returned to Cynthia. "Who're we having?" he asked.

Cynthia typed on the keyboard, her brows furrowing as she squinted at the screen. "Nevaeh Carr is scheduled for six, and it's about that time now, so I guess she'll be here?" She leaned back against the magenta cushion of her chair, absentmindedly raising her pen to her lips.

"Nevaeh Carr…" Sean pondered the name, trying to recall a face to match it. "I don't have any little ones named Nevaeh," he remarked. Parents often booked private lessons for their children's advancement. Sometimes, parents believed that one-on-one sessions with Sean would increase their daughters' chances of landing lead roles in the annual Nutcracker performance. There were even instances where women in Sweetgum paid for classes just to be in close proximity to *him* as they wanted to relieve him of his single status.

"No, she's an adult," Cynthia chimed in with a yawn, scrolling through her phone. "If she doesn't show up within the next ten minutes, should we lock up?" She stretched, and a satisfying pop resonated from her back.

"That's the policy. Direct her to the practice room if she comes in." He turned on his heel, heading there to wait.

Leaning against the wall, Sean downed his water, only to be interrupted by a sudden realization. "Nevaeh Carr," he pondered. He'd met her briefly in the past. He was with Justin when he saw her. She was a friend of Justin's girlfriend, and he had briefly interacted with her. However, Sean couldn't picture any distinctive features or details about her. "Hmm…" He wondered why she would want dance lessons. Was there a special occasion, or was this some scheme to hook up with him?

He hoped the latter was false. Though 'lesson dates' brought good business, they usually went nowhere and wasted the time of both him and those who'd booked them. Sean prided himself on maintaining focus when it came to his business, not only for ethical reasons but also due to his unique situation. He didn't have time for relationships. Tia meant the world to him, and after her came dance. Bringing a woman into his life would disrupt his order.

Either way, Sean hoped Nevaeh's desire for lessons was solely based on her interest in dance.

"Hi?"

He ceased all thinking when he raised his eyes to the speaker of the voice. "Hey," Sean slowly put down his water bottle.

Nevaeh stood in the doorway, clad in gray sweatpants and a snug, cropped hoodie that accentuated her toned figure. Her lustrous black hair was elegantly fashioned into a sleek bun, but what truly captivated Sean's attention were her intriguing eyes, framed by perfectly arched eyebrows, adding an appealing charm to her already captivating face. Her warm, glowing brown skin had a radiant quality, and a playful smile adorned her lips, reflecting a glossy sheen under the bright fluorescent lights of the room.

Sean stiffened as she cautiously entered, sneakers squeaking against the waxed wood. He didn't remember her looking like this.

She pursed her lips slightly and made her way toward him, her hand slipping into the pocket of her cropped hoodie. "You're Sean, right?" she inquired, her voice tinged with a hint of uncertainty.

Nestled between her fingers, she held a card that she quickly stowed away, her other hand rubbing her arm nervously.

Sean sensed his own momentary hesitation and blinked, refocusing his attention. "Yes, that's me. I'm Sean," he responded, offering her a warm smile as he positioned himself beneath the central light fixture of the room. Their voices seemed to reverberate within the spacious surroundings. "And you must be Nevaeh?" he continued, extending his hand towards her, his gaze locking with her sparkling eyes.

"Yup—I mean yes. Yes, I'm Nevaeh, and I am here… to dance," she squeaked out a laugh, taking his hand and shaking it firmly.

Whoa. Sean was surprised by her strength. Her hand, though smaller than his, had quite the grip. There was also a level of warmth to it. That and dampness. Was she sweating? *She's really nervous.* He could tell that much. "Ah, here to learn how to dance?" He decided to keep things light, eager to ease her first-class jitters.

"Yes, I am. I really am." She'd been carrying a small backpack on one shoulder. She peeled it off and tossed the bag aside, causing a crash that startled Sean.

Sean noticed the tiny jump she tried to hide. "You didn't break anything in there, right?" he nodded toward the bag, now growing concerned. Was he intimidating? What could he do to relax her? She had not struck him as angsty on their first encounter. But then again, Sean could hardly remember what she'd been like back then. In fact, he couldn't remember anything. Not right now. Not with her here in his studio. What was going on with him? He could admit that she was attractive, but would leave it at that. She was his student, and that was it.

Nevaeh's finger pushed some stray hair behind her ear, then used her hand to flatten the strands against her scalp. "Hopefully not. I'm sorry. I swear I'm not usually like this." Her hands folding and unfolding with a touch of unease.

"Okay. If you're nervous, it's normal. Seems dancing's new to you and I'm a new person." He resisted the urge to reach for her shoulder and instead set his hands on his hips. "But don't worry. We're going to be all right. I'm going to teach you what you need to know and you'll learn it just fine. You seem pretty sharp," he winked.

Nevaeh appeared preoccupied, setting her gaze on the wall rather than on him. "We're going to be all right..." she repeated, cracking her knuckles.

Sean examined her face. "Nevaeh?" What on earth was she thinking? He taught children as young as two, but even they remained mentally present for lessons. Toddlers tended to stay engaged when activities piqued their interest. Maybe getting started would keep her with him. "All right, how about we hop in? Oh, but before that, can you tell me your experience?" He stretched his shoulder by straightening one arm across his upper chest and hooking the other under it. "Follow my lead while we chat."

"Yeah, yeah, okay." Nevaeh took a few seconds to inspect his form, then replicated it. She easily got the stretch, but that was expected.

"Ready to tell me your experience?" Sean coaxed, dipping his chin slightly. He caught himself, embarrassed for utilizing tactics reserved for his niece. Lowering his face and lifting his eyeballs always worked when Tia grew stubborn. Nevaeh was nervous, not a child.

She switched her arms when he did, blowing a sigh. "I have no dance experience," she admitted dejectedly.

"Okay. Not even at parties or for fun? Don't dance to music?" Sean got low for the hip flexor stretch.

Once again, Nevaeh watched first before following. She nearly tipped over with a squeal after positioning her knee, but Sean held her arm to keep her upright. The squeal caught him off guard. He hid a smile at this reaction.

"Thank you," she huffed, pulling her jacket onto her shoulder. "So, we went from easy arm stretches to big-time moves in ten seconds? Is that how this class works?" she shot him a glance while wobbling.

Sean detected a lack of coordination. Most students got through warm-ups with no difficulty. He'd thought the same would go for Nevaeh, but her struggle was apparent. *She's clumsy.* "Oh no. These aren't big-time moves. This is a stretch too. It's pretty common. You must have seen it on TV, right?"

With a gasp, she fell to her side but shot up immediately. "I knew that." She pulled up her sleeves to her elbows. "Is that all? I think I've stretched enough." Her fingers pinched the chest of her jacket, puffing it out.

Sean stood, too, undoing his pose effortlessly. "We usually stretch for at least five minutes, but if you're ready to jump right in, I guess we can." He took note of her refusal for eye contact. Nevaeh was easy to read. He could deduce there was a ton of pride stacked in that slender body.

The young woman clapped once. "All right, let's do it then. I'm ready to get to the stuff. Oh, I need to learn how to waltz, by the way. Is that okay?" she snapped her fingers like it had just occurred to her.

Sean allowed his smile to spread. "That's perfectly fine."

CHAPTER FOUR

*N*evaeh observed her dance teacher with a mix of resentment and admiration as he patiently explained the fundamentals. His unwavering gaze met hers, and he took his time explaining what lay ahead. She nodded in acknowledgment, tilting her head up and then lowering it to show her comprehension. Folding one arm and bending the other at the elbow, she placed her palm against her cheek, mirroring his instructions. Despite the hour being far from over, beads of sweat formed on her brow, prompted by the relentless summer heat, as she pushed herself through the exercises.

Aw Brands, she thought, requesting that Sean demonstrate once more. It seemed simple in theory and gave that impression, too. Nevaeh knew herself, though. This 'kickball change' or whatever he'd called it would blow up in her face once she made her attempt.

She rubbed an eye in exasperation. Her love for Brandi was infinite and, most times, their bond was fulfilling. However, Nevaeh despised Brandi's impressive knowledge of her schedule. The woman had booked these lessons for every Tuesday evening until the wedding, with no consultation from Nevaeh. Nothing clashed, and no adjustments were required. How touching? Half of her battled the joyful tears sitting within her eyelids while the other fought tears of frustration. Not only had Brandi successfully scheduled lessons at a time of convenience, but had paid for them too. Failure was simply not an option. Her best friend had gone out of her way for this.

"Okay, no. Just relax and step-step kick. You can do it. Come on," said the instructor. *Sean,* she'd seen him around town now and then. He had some skill. Not only that, but he had talent, too. And he was quite handsome. But she wouldn't think about that. His moves were smooth and precise; no action went to waste. She'd pin him at around six feet tall. He had lean muscles that were defined through his dance trousers. But she wouldn't think about that, either. The fade of his haircut was fresh, and his face was clean-shaven. Under the white lights, his dark brown skin tone gleamed. 'Neat' was a word she'd associate with him. Welcoming too. The man possessed a calm, pleasant demeanor that was refreshing in this new setting. His studio was nothing to sneeze at. She felt like a celebrity preparing for a tour.

Nevaeh put her all into the moves. "Step, step-woah!" She slipped on her heel, but Sean caught her. He straightened her with firm hands on her torso and back. "Sorry. Your floors are slippery. You should look into fixing that." She cursed herself for messing up so colossally. There were *five* months until the wedding and her classes were booked every week until then. It seemed like ample time, but Nevaeh had no intention of attending all of them. Her hope was to heighten her skills in three months, maximum. That way, Brandi could be refunded for the remaining months of classes.

"Right. The floors are slippery," Sean agreed facetiously.

Nevaeh tried to read him. She saw his joking mien and blood rose to her cheeks. "Hey!"

Sean dragged a hand down his sweaty face. "You ready to try that again, Nevaeh?"

"You were laughing at me." *How horrible!* A professional deemed her efforts worthy of ridicule. She knew this would happen. Her skills were pathetic. Was she hopeless? She couldn't be. This had to work for Brandi—her best friend believed in her. Nevaeh would die before she let her down. Yes, her inner monologue was a bit intense, but Brandi's happiness meant everything.

Sean shook his head, his hand gesturing in a reassuring manner. "No, no. I wasn't laughing, I promise. It's not like that," he quickly clarified. With two fingers framing his chin, he paused for a moment, gathering his thoughts. "It's just that... you seem to be in denial," he gently pointed out, his tone filled with understanding.

Nevaeh recoiled. "About what?"

He did not expound. "Let's just go over this another time, okay? I think you're getting close. You just need to focus on your two feet and then your legs when you kick," he hovered both arms around her like a barricade. "You got a lot going on up here and with your neck and your head, but you don't need to do that. We're just stepping and kicking. So, let's break it down. One step. Do that for me?" He showed her.

Nevaeh would ignore his comment for now. She needed to focus. "One step," she stomped her left foot.

Sean nodded. "Okay, yes, but do it like me. Stomp softly on one foot, come on, let's go," he did so again.

Her bun loosened as she followed. "Like this?"

"Yeah, perfect. Now do it with your other foot," Sean provided instructions and studied their reflection.

Nevaeh completed the rudimentary direction. "I know I'm not the best you've taught, but you don't have to go this slow," she grumbled.

Sean's snort was subtle, but she heard it.

"Do you think I can't see when you laugh that way?" Nevaeh wasn't annoyed this time. Something about his hidden amusement intrigued her. His attitude so far was too motivating to label him a jerk.

"Nevaeh, I swear I'm not laughing *at* you. Teaching you is just fun," he confessed pleasantly. "And I know you're capable of a lot, but sometimes breaking it down to the smallest parts helps even the best dancers," he lowered his body. "Can you do that?"

Nevaeh dropped with more force, almost losing balance. She swallowed a scream that came with the rush. "You're lucky you have a nice laugh," she commented.

Sean froze temporarily, then cleared his throat. "Thank you," he went on with the lesson. "All right, dip gently. You added a bit too much energy. Let me see you. Nice and gentle,"

His tender approach was both encouraging and demeaning. Nevaeh was not sure how to take it, but she admired his persistence.

Soon she was stepping and dipping, grinning with pride. "Ha! So much for bumbling klutz, huh?" Maybe this was doable. She had started at zero but reached one at last. She swung her hips for flavor. "Got a bit of a spring in my waist. Don't mind me," she giggled like a child who'd discovered a new trick.

Sean appeared at her back, holding her shoulders, which jerked uncontrollably. "You're widening your stance. Remember, feet together. Oh, and your hips are popping too strongly. Also, your back is arched." He carefully altered her formation with cautious palms.

With every adjustment, Nevaeh lost control. When he straightened her back, her head jolted backward and bumped into his nose.

"Ah!" Sean covered his face, tottering away.

"Sorry!" Nevaeh whirled on her heel to help, but slid right to the floor onto her side with the motion. Her shoulder crashed when she landed and a shriek left her mouth.

"Oh gosh," Sean released his nose to bend over. He extended a hand when she recovered from stun and helped her to her feet. "Accidents happen with first-timers." His positive attitude remained unaffected.

Nevaeh, on the other hand, was ready to call it a day. "Ugh!" She looked at the ceiling in despondence, its blinding lights burning her pupils. "I'm messing up *so* bad. Look, I'm sorry. I swear I'm better than this," she lied through her teeth. Sure, her friends knew of her challenge, but that did not mean that others had to. She tried to maintain a confident persona around new people. That went for this dancing guy, too, even if he did seem understanding.

"That's okay, I don't mind. You're here to learn. My role is to teach you, remember? I've had tons of students come in knowing nothing about dance. I just try my best, and we work through things together. It's supposed to be fun. So, relax and let's dance," he went back to stepping. "See that? You can do this, right?"

By now, loose strands of her hair hung around her head. She ripped off her hairband and pulled her wisps through it in a pony-tail. "I mean, yeah. I was just doing that a while ago, wasn't I?" she stomped her feet then swung her hips.

"No, no," Sean stopped and got behind her again. He held her waist, then reached for her knees, tapping them. She would not think about the flutters that she felt in her belly. "No stomping. Stepping Nevaeh, stepping. Gentle steps. We went over this. And what you were doing earlier was a bit too... um... uncontained. So, we're going to bring control back to things because dance is all about controlling our bodies. Now go on. Step, step, step, step," he maintained equanimity even as her body swayed against her will. He simply made adjustments by shifting her when necessary. "Right. I think we're ready for the kick," he slid aside. "Want to show me how you kick?"

Nevaeh huffed but kicked high, her foot almost colliding with his face. "Sorry!"

Sean had fortunately dodged it. He steadied her body after the act, accepting her apology. "Okay, so that's a beautiful high kick, but we're going to keep our legs close to the ground for this. Just a simple kick forward like this." After executing two steps, the man made a slight angle between his right leg and body. "See?"

Nevaeh, eager to get this, rushed in on thumping feet. That was until Sean gave a reminder. *Step lightly.* She tried to do so and kicked forward. Only that her kick was the opposite of his. Nevaeh thrust her leg like a striker in a soccer match. "Like that?"

"No, no, but you're getting there. Gently Nevaeh, gently and small," Sean demonstrated with ease and kept going, cueing her in with a count. She missed every one and came in off-timing. He tried again by clapping to assist.

Overwhelmed with emotions, Nevaeh came to a halt, her hands instinctively covering her face as she tried to hide her feelings. Her body language revealed the depth of her vulnerability in that moment.

"Nevaeh? Are you okay?" Sean's warm presence drew closer, his hand gently resting on her shoulder. Concern filled his voice as he reached out to comfort her.

Determined not to give up, Nevaeh pushed aside her negative thoughts. She reminded herself that time was precious, and she couldn't afford to waste this class dwelling on her emotions. "I'm fine," she shook away her sadness and got in the groove. "Step, step kick. Like this, right?"

Sean once again gave his input on how to improve. He touched her shoulders as she polished her moves and then commended her. "Okay, so we can try a few more steps for these last ten minutes, and then we'll put them all together," he clasped his hands at his chest, not a slither of agitation detectable.

Nevaeh gawked in amazement at his tolerance. She might have lost it in his shoes. "Okay," she braced herself for the worst.

Ten minutes were up, and Nevaeh was puffing. She listened to Sean's counts while side-stepping, but kicked her own heel and fell to her shoulder. She yelped on the landing but shuffled to her hands and knees.

"Oh boy," said Sean after clapping. He squatted in front of her. "Are you okay?" just his tone reassured her. His deep brown eyes held concern.

She sighed and stood up, rubbing her shoulder. "At this rate, I'll end up in a full body cast before the wedding."

"That won't happen," he said. "And we have plenty of time to learn a basic waltz. You're going to be fine. Just in this hour, you made tons of improvements." His positivity was unmatched. It put her at ease, but only a smidge. "Trust me, by the time we're done, you'll be a boss on the dance floor. It'll take time and patience, but this is a start. Don't fret."

Nevaeh's irritation dwindled. She swayed with a hand on her arm and opened her mouth to respond, but a small voice cut her off.

"Look at this!"

Nevaeh startled at the little girl in the doorway. The child wore a paper crown and carried a notebook. Her doe eyes and round face spelled innocence, and her adorable bun made her all the more precious.

She watched in awe as the child met Sean with a skip and giggles. Her tiny hands peeled the book open to Sean's face. She tiptoed to reach him, boasting an accomplishment. To that, the dance teacher gasped in wonder, commending her work. He planted a kiss on her chubby cheek, and they both bounced with glee.

This interaction, though endearing, caused unease to settle in Nevaeh. The reason was unclear, but she took that as her cue to exit. After a rushed thank you to Sean, she sped-walked through the door with aching limbs and muscles.

CHAPTER FIVE

Sean leaned into the car, reaching across the backseat to fasten Tia's seatbelt. He made sure it was snug and secure, double-checking for her safety.

The weekend raced by, leaving him with a whirlwind of classes, housework, and joyous moments shared with his niece. As the school year drew to a close, Tia's boundless energy overflowed, fueled by the excitement of her friends' summer plans. Although unicorn rides and dates with a prince were out of reach, their to-do list brimmed with beach visits and hiking expeditions, and Sean eagerly offered his assistance. Tia, a true adventure seeker, kindled his pride as he wholeheartedly encouraged her passion for quests and discoveries.

As she belted out the bridge of a popular song, he swung her door shut with a playful flourish. Sean absentmindedly joined in the singing while settling into the driver's seat. Getting comfortable, he conscientiously pulled on his own seatbelt for safety. "All right, time for dinner," he announced, ready to embark on their next adventure.

One of the things he loved about Sweetgum was its tranquil atmosphere. The absence of cars on the road made for a smooth journey. Sean drove past humble bungalows, duplexes, and a four-story condominium before making a turn. In a front yard, a couple of children were engaged in a lively game of frisbee, their laughter filling the air as he passed by. It was the Masons' house. He remembered they had recently welcomed a new addition to their family—a dog. Since then, the children seemed to be inseparable from their furry companion. Although he wasn't particularly fond of dogs himself, he couldn't deny the adorable charm when Tia had asked him about it.

Her curiosity knew no bounds, as was typical for a seven-year-old, always inquisitive and filled with wonder. This week, Tia had developed an intense fascination with Nevaeh after walking in on Sean's lesson. Initially, he had assumed that Tia paid no attention to Nevaeh, but their drive home proved otherwise. In just seven minutes, Tia bombarded him with an onslaught of questions. Sean, opting for evasive responses, kept his answers vague, explaining that Nevaeh was simply a new student with a strong desire to learn. He patiently reassured Tia that there was nothing more to it. However, Tia remained unconvinced. Her argument was that Nevaeh was beautiful, and therefore, she must be Sean's love interest.

Sean had not known how else to tell her that looks meant nothing in this scenario, so had opted to shrug her off. Eventually, she'd moved on, and he was happy to do the same.

Sean squeezed his steering wheel as the sky slowly turned orange. Six pm had long gone, but daylight remained. He entered a new street, joining traffic with a lump in his throat. Had he moved on? Not in the slightest.

From the second Nevaeh had raced out his door, he'd thought of her. Not only because she was unique in her baffling lack of coordination but also due to her vibe. Her frustration over the simplest move, though sad, had charmed him. His last interaction with a woman he was interested in was long ago, but that brief lesson with Nevaeh brought his flirt out, which was strange because he had not intended to tease and have fun with her. Sean distinctly remembered vowing to maintain professionalism the second she'd entered. And though, for the most part, he'd achieved his goal, he'd teetered into 'flirting' territory at least once or twice. Regardless, he enjoyed the experience and believed that she did too, except for the moments when extreme annoyance crossed her face.

He recalled the sting of her head crushing his nose, though the damage wasn't severe. It hurt a ton more than he'd led on, but Sean refused to add guilt to her agitation. He believed that everyone had a dancer within them, and with effort and dedication, they could unleash that part of themselves. However, most people weren't willing to put in the necessary work. What was Nevaeh's drive? That question frequently occupied his thoughts when he considered her. He concluded that his wandering thoughts stemmed from an interest in his student's motivation. The only thing was that their lesson kept replaying in his mind, unable to be forgotten.

Her slip-ups, his rescues, her whining, his encouragement— these moments intertwined in their dance lesson. He couldn't deny the joy his profession brought to his soul, but this time, the enjoyment surpassed the normal amount. Sean found himself wishing that Tia hadn't interrupted their session. Nevaeh's mouth had been open, ready to reply, but his niece's sudden entrance had shut her down. Since then, she had shifted drastically, her demeanor changing in an instant. Her hasty goodbye and abrupt exit constantly replayed in his mind during idle moments.

"Yay, grandma's house!" Tia brought him back to reality with her bubbly exclamation.

Sean parked his car and turned off the engine, preparing to exit. "Ready to grab a bite?" he asked, unfastening his seatbelt. He needed a distraction from his swirling thoughts. Reflecting on his interactions with Nevaeh felt pointless and strange. As he had told Tia, she was just another student, and he should treat her as such.

"Uh-huh," Tia exclaimed eagerly as she bolted out of the car and made her way to the front gate. The porch illuminated as she opened the gate, revealing Sean's mother standing there. "Grandma, we're here!" Tia exclaimed joyfully, rushing forward to embrace her.

"Ooh, my perfect princess! Look at you!" Sean's mother swaddled Tia in a loving embrace. She showered kisses on the girl's forehead as they swayed from left to right.

Sean balanced the bowls of salad and barbecue chicken in his hands, the foil covering them to keep them warm. He had retrieved them from the passenger seat moments earlier. "How you doing, Mom?" He greeted her as they met by the door. Leaning down, he placed a gentle kiss on her forehead after she let go of Tia.

His mother tenderly placed her hand on his cheek, leaning in to press her lips against his nose with a playful "*mwa.*" A mischievous grin spread across her face, eliciting a giggle from Tia. Faint wrinkles appeared near the corners of her mouth, but Sean refused to acknowledge them. She never referred to herself as "old." In her eyes, she was "fine" – like a fine wine aged gracefully on a rack. The strands of gray in her hair were mere reflections of her wisdom and experience. Tonight, they were concealed beneath the white Nonbongoy head wrap she wore. Even in retirement, she remained dedicated to presenting herself with elegance and style. Now, more than ever, she looked absolutely stunning.

Minutes later, they settled down in the kitchen. His mom added the salad and barbecue to the lineup of dishes on the table, apologizing for possibly overcooking. The aroma of mac and cheese and rice wafted from the stove. Despite the narrow table, it was filled to capacity with a feast. Throughout his childhood, he had enjoyed countless glorious meals in this very kitchen. His parents were true culinary masters, and he couldn't help but boast about their cooking skills. His mom, in particular, had a remarkable talent for infusing each dish with exceptional flavors through her impeccable seasoning abilities.

"It's okay, Grandma. We never say it, but Uncle Sean and I love it when you give us extra food," Tia said, taking her seat next to Sean as she twirled her fork in anticipation. Her gaze wandered around the kitchen, her twists bouncing with her movements. "Where's Grandpa? Did he fall asleep before dinner again?" She attempted to impale a piece of freshly baked bread with her fork, but Sean gently stopped her, reminding her that they hadn't said grace yet.

"Oh, he'll be here once he catches a whiff of this. He spent all day mowing the lawn, you see. The man's exhausted," Sean's mom explained, finding a spot for the additional platters by rearranging the others. She brought them forward and took her seat. "But you might want to dig in before he arrives because we all know how voracious Grandpa can be," she added, directing her comment to Tia.

Tia gasped. "You're right. Let's pray right now before he eats everything here. I swear Grandpa eats more than you, Uncle Sean. Why don't you eat as much if you're a man, too?" She playfully used her fork to scrape her empty plate, eliciting laughter from the adults.

Sean ruffled her hair affectionately. "I suppose I'm just not as greedy as Grandpa," he said with a smile. As footsteps approached from the stairs, he leaned in to kiss Tia's forehead, preparing for the arrival of their hungry family member.

"Hold on, the whole family's already here?" his dad's voice echoed through the kitchen as he stumbled in, rubbing his sleepy eyes and clutching a newspaper. His dramatic gasp filled the room as he noticed Tia sitting there. "And the princess herself is here and didn't even bother to greet me?" he exclaimed, feigning offense.

Tia rose from her chair. "I didn't see you when I came, Grandpa. Princess Tia makes mistakes, too." She gave him a hug when he cackled.

"All right, everyone, let's sit down and eat," Sean said with a smile. He couldn't help but appreciate Tia's sense of humor. Was there ever a more perfect child? Without a doubt, Tia was the best, the "GOAT" as she would sometimes say.

"Honey, go wash your hands and join us," his mother instructed his dad. Sean felt the hunger gnawing at his stomach. Sundays were usually more relaxed compared to weekdays, but his meager lunch of leftover pizza had been too long ago.

They said grace, and the aroma of the delicious food filled the room as the family eagerly dug into their plates. Merry chewing sounds and compliments to the chefs filled the air, creating a joyful atmosphere. It was safe to say that they had once again outdone themselves for another Sunday dinner.

Tia's plate was already half-empty when she reached for her napkin to wipe away the grease from her lips. She looked up at Sean with curious eyes. "Uncle Sean, are you going to tell Grandma and Grandpa about Nevaeh now?" she asked, her voice filled with anticipation and her eyes with mischief.

As the question about Nevaeh caught Sean off guard, a small chip from the bone he was munching on flew down his throat, causing him to choke. His mother, sensing the urgency, quickly sprang into action. "Nevaeh?" she exclaimed; her voice filled with concern. "Oh, my goodness! Sean, honey, drink some water! Quickly!" She hurriedly got up from her seat, grabbed his water, and pressed it to his lips, urging him to drink.

Despite some water spilling on his band T-shirt, Sean managed to regain his composure. He cleared his throat and took a few more sips of water to ease the discomfort. "I-I'm fine," he rasped, his voice still recovering. His parents and Tia continued to stare at him, waiting for an explanation. Sean composed himself and asked, "Ehem, why would I tell them about Nevaeh, T?"

"Who's Nevaeh?" asked his dad with a mouth full of rice. He'd devoured his seconds a while ago. His appetite seemed opposite to his physique. The man was slender, tall, and in good shape aside from the gut he'd grown.

Tia beamed mischievously. "Wow, Grandpa, I'm glad you asked because she's actually pretty special to Uncle Sean," she said with a twinkle in her eyes, just like the sly foxes in fairytales, except much cuter because she was an adorable little girl.

Sean cleared his throat in a vain attempt to regain composure.

"She's not any more special than any other student, okay?" he replied, his voice slightly strained. His heart rate seemed to increase with each passing moment. Why couldn't Tia let go of this topic? And why did she choose now to bring up Nevaeh again? A nagging thought surfaced in his mind, wondering if Tia had deliberately planned this, waiting for the perfect moment to bring up Nevaeh and torment him. Mission accomplished, he thought, shaking his head. "She's just a new student of mine. She happens to be friends with Justin's girlfriend."

"What's this? A connection?" Tia pointed her two forefingers at the ceiling and then joined them. With an exaggerated wink and a wiggle of her little brows, she shot Sean a playful grin, as if she had just uncovered the juiciest secret.

"You're too adorable." Sean threw a napkin at her while his parents watched adoringly. "She's just a student that T, for some reason, is obsessed with."

"Why?" his father cut himself another slice of mac and cheese. "Is she your type?"

"Yes!" said Tia.

"No," Sean protested, his face growing warmer than a chili pepper. "She really is just a student. Tia has an overactive imagination from all those romantic comedies she watches when she visits you without me, Mom," he retorted, pouting at his wide-eyed mother.

"Me?" His mother hit her chest melodramatically. "You're the one who reads her too many princess stories. How do they all end, Sean? Princess marries the prince and happily ever after. This is on you, son. Don't drag your momma where she doesn't belong." She bit her chicken when they all bellowed with laughter.

Later, Tia and his dad flicked through channels in the living room while Sean helped his mom clean up.

His mom's elbows were immersed in soapy water, her hands diligently scrubbing the dishes. As she worked, she hummed a familiar hymn from their church, her gaze fixed on the window, where the darkness of the night had already settled in.

Sean rinsed at her side. He chucked their forks in the drainer, then poured what felt like a gallon of water out of a pot. "So, Mom, how did I do with the twists in Tia's hair? Did they turn out all right, or should I leave the intricate styles to you?" he asked, a hint of playfulness in his voice.

"Ha." She scraped the bristles of her cleaning brush against the macaroni dish. "You did a great job, Sean. I'm impressed." Her voice trailed off as she exhaled, her mood taking a downward turn. "You've adapted better than any of us imagined." She let water pour into the pan before meticulously checking its corners for any remnants of gunk.

Sean rested the pot on the bottom shelf of their drainer. "Thank you," he took the pan when she was through.

"She's growing up so quickly; it's truly amazing to witness," Sean's mom remarked, her voice filled with both pride and nostalgia as she switched back to using a sponge for the plates. "It feels like just yesterday she was so tiny, a little baby," she added, her eyes taking on a distant, wistful look. "And now..." The sound of Tia's infectious giggles echoed from the living room, bringing a smile to both of their faces. "She resembles her so much," she continued, handing Sean the plate full of suds. "Not just in her appearance, but in the way she acts and moves with such vibrancy. Oh, Sean, she reminds me so much of your sister, it almost overwhelms me," she said softly, bowing her head and focusing on the task of washing.

Sean grew quiet, listening as the jabbering from his dad and Tia overpowered the sound of running water.

"I think she'd be proud if she was still here. Proud of not just Tia's growth, but of your own strength and determination. You've stepped up and surpassed all expectations. I couldn't be prouder of you. And let me tell you, she would have loved you even more, which is truly remarkable considering the special place you already held in her heart," his mother said, scrubbing the plate with determination. "Now, let's wrap up these dishes and join in on the board game fun before those two sneak a head-start on us."

"Yes, ma'am," Sean took her words to heart. None of them could speak on behalf of his sister, but he hoped she was smiling from above. It touched him when his mom cheered on his efforts.

Sean nodded with a grateful smile. "Thank you, Mom. Your words mean a lot to me. I hope she's looking down on us and feeling proud, too." The warmth in his heart grew as he finished up the last of the dishes, appreciating his mother's unwavering support and encouragement.

CHAPTER SIX

As Nevaeh sat inside Rochelle's Old Fashion Diner, she shifted with discomfort from her aches. It didn't help that she fell a few times during last week's dance lessons, which worsened her pain. Luckily, the recent falls weren't as bad as before; they were more like adding to her existing discomfort rather than causing fresh injuries. *How could a person be so clumsy?*

She made a deliberate decision to keep both hands firmly placed on the table instead of automatically reaching for her sore shoulders. At the same time, Rochelle stayed behind the counter, dutifully getting their drinks ready, while the rest of the book club members found their cozy spots in the comfortable U-shaped booth located towards the back of the diner. The vivid red leather cushions produced a soft squeak with every movement the women made, contributing a lively element to the ambiance.

Their book club meetings always had a great turnout. As Mrs. Zhang, the owner of Sweet and Spicy Chinese Palace, frequently said, "It would require nothing short of Armageddon itself to prevent us from attending." The atmosphere was simply infectious, and the allure of the books added to the appeal. "Lost Souls" was so good that Nevaeh couldn't put it down. She stayed up past midnight reading it the night before. Nevaeh was captivated by the love redemption trope in the book and eagerly followed the lovers' journey.

"Do you want to hear my thoughts on that?" Mrs. Andrews had a shawl draped over her blouse for the evening, and she gently tapped her ringed fingers on the red table to settle them down. The age gap between Nevaeh, her friends, and the spirited group of older women known as the "hit-and-run" club, aptly named for their propensity to knock people out of the way during their energetic morning speed-walking sessions, never hindered their ability to engage in conversation. Whenever they gathered, it felt like old friends coming together again. The older women, in particular, had plenty of stories to share, and they never failed to entertain Nevaeh and the other younger members with their tales. Kim, their final book club member, was absent tonight as she was traveling with her fiancé, Malik.

"What's on your mind, hon?" Rochelle asked as she approached, balancing a wide tray filled with an assortment of teas. Her braids hung low as she carefully positioned the beverages on the table. A chorus of grateful "thank you's" followed her as she made her way back behind the counter.

"She asked what you were thinking but didn't stick around to hear it," Mrs. Bridges wheezed on a laugh with her elbow nudging Mrs. Andrews. Her faux locs shook with her energetic motions.

Everyone joined in on the laughter. The seating arrangement was the same as it always was, with the older women occupying one side while the younger ones sat on the other. Mrs. Craskin, as always, held her place at the head of the table, reaching out to grab her mint tea from the tray of labeled flasks.

"Oh, Mrs. Bridges always manages to find a joke even when there isn't one," Mrs. Andrews playfully nudged her aside with her elbow. She blew on her tea to cool it before passionately sharing her opinions about the heroine in their story and Mrs. Craskin complained about the heroine.

"Ah! Mrs. Craskin, I am so glad you mentioned the heroine's complacency because I was thinking the same thing," Joanne exclaimed with fervor. She pointed emphatically at the cover of her book, her passion igniting. "Why does she expect him to fix all of her problems? They're both lost souls together, aren't they? Just as she supported his growth while he found himself," each woman listened intently, captivated by her words, "she should expect support, not a miracle. She can lean on him, but burdening that poor man with the weight of her recovery on his shoulders is unfair!" Joanne slammed her hand on the table, causing their cups to tremble under the force. Normally, they would wait for Rochelle, but she had encouraged them to start without her as something in the kitchen had kept her busy.

Nevaeh imagined the pain of heavy loads on her throbbing shoulders as the women snapped their fingers unanimously. "I've got to agree, there. His poor aching shoulders." It took everything in her not to whimper.

"You okay there, Nev? You've been a little off since we got here." Brandi gently patted her on the back.

Nevaeh inwardly cursed as she felt the weight of the gathered attention on her. Usually, she welcomed the curious gazes of the group, but tonight, being the center of intrigue, felt overwhelming. "Oh, I'm fine, really," she replied with a forced nonchalance. "Just contemplating work-related matters and such. You know how it is." She took a sip of her tea, only to recoil with a yelp as the scalding heat caught her off guard, almost causing her to spit out the liquid she had gathered in her mouth.

"Who's bothering you at work?" Courtney asked, her brow furrowing with confusion. "I thought Mrs. Greendale was nice. Is she overworking you planning all the Sweetgum events, Nev? You do look a little rundown tonight." As she spoke, the rest of the table leaned in, their eyes fixed on Nevaeh, assessing her with intensity.

Nevaeh avoided their eyes. "No one. I've been exercising a lot, okay? That's why I may seem a little rundown." She briefly thought back to her at-home dance practice last night before showering. She'd done a few steps in front of her mirror but had failed miserably.

"Oh yeah, the dance lessons, right?" Brandi's brown eyes lit up, a twinkle shimmering in them. "How are they going? I've been so busy planning that I haven't gotten around to asking for updates. Tomorrow's your third class, right?"

While Nevaeh stammered, Joanne caught everyone up to speed on why these lessons were so important. Of course, she sprinkled in a few stories to depict the severity of Nevaeh's clumsiness. "Yeah, tomorrow's the third class and as for how it's been going?"

Nevaeh's left shoulder throbbed, a constant reminder of her fall last week. During that incident, both Sean and his adorable daughter had rushed to her aid. Sean, as always, had been patient, kind, and understanding, like an angel, even when Nevaeh had become upset about her clumsy stumble. Tia, Sean's sweet little princess, had been just as charming. At first, Nevaeh had been reluctant to accept a child correcting her mistakes, but Tia's cuteness melted away any frustration. The child had initially observed from the doorway before offering some advice. While a few suggestions had been helpful, most had led to disastrous outcomes. Nevaeh couldn't understand why Tia and Sean hadn't scolded her for every mistake she made last week. They truly seemed like saints.

Brandi dipped her chin and raised both eyes in expectation, the pause between Nevaeh's own question and answer growing inordinately long. "Uh-huh?"

"Can't you remember, dear?" said Mrs. Andrews, lifting her cup of peppermint tea to her mouth.

Nevaeh cleared her throat. "The lessons have been fine. Amazing even. If I'd known that dance classes were all it would take to fix my two left feet, I would have booked some a long time ago." She popped off the plastic covering on her disposable cup to blow on her steaming chamomile tea.

"All right!" Joanne exclaimed, initiating a round of applause by clapping her hands together with a wide grin.

"You go, girl! I can't wait to see you tearing up the dance floor," Courtney exclaimed, her fingers fidgeting with the watch on her silver necklace. The necklace hung against her exposed chest, peeking through the stylish design of her camisole. She wore her denim jacket, casually rolled up to her elbows.

"I can't even imagine Nevaeh busting out moves that don't make me want to call an ambulance," Joanne continued with her string of jokes, clearly on a roll. Nevaeh felt her face flush with embarrassment, hiding her shame behind her palm.

"All right, Joanne, let's not tease every time we talk about her dancing, okay?" Brandi chided, her tone firm. "Nevaeh is putting in a lot of effort and making steady progress, so let's do our best to support her."

A warm, fuzzy sensation flooded Nevaeh's insides, but at the same time, a sickening guilt settled in her stomach. Why did Brandi have to be such a sweetheart? Dealing with this situation was already challenging enough, and she didn't need the added weight of kindness making her shame worse when she lied. Nevaeh responded to Brandi's comment, trying to shift the focus. "Thanks, Brands," she said, mustering a smile. "On a completely different note, I'm really excited about Matt's visit next week. Did I mention that to you guys? He's taking a break before his next trip." If they continued discussing her dancing, she feared she might break under the pressure.

"Oh, nice!" the women chimed in, sharing her enthusiasm and voicing their happiness for her.

Joanne, always the one to speak her mind, furrowed her brow and leaned in closer. "Nevaeh, can we talk for a moment?" she asked, her tone laced with concern.

Nevaeh glanced at Joanne and nodded, signaling her willingness to listen. Sensing something serious, the rest of the group quieted down, their curious eyes fixed on the two friends.

Joanne took a deep breath before speaking, her voice steady. "Nevaeh, we all know how much you care about Matt, but let's be real here. He's a musician, always on the road, and it seems like he's frequently stood you up when he said he was coming. Are you sure this is what you want?"

Nevaeh felt her cheeks flush with a mix of embarrassment and frustration. She understood their concern, but she didn't want them to think she was investing too much in a relationship that wasn't even there. She took a moment to collect her thoughts before responding. With this topic change, it seemed like she jumped straight from the frying pan into the fire.

"Joanne, I appreciate your concern, really, I do," Nevaeh said, her voice filled with sincerity. "But you have to understand that Matt and I are just having fun. We're not in a serious relationship, and my feelings aren't engaged in that way. We enjoy each other's company, and I see him more as a friend than anything else."

The group exchanged glances, their expressions softening with understanding. Brandi reached out and squeezed Nevaeh's hand gently. "We just want to make sure you're not getting hurt, Nevaeh. We care about you, and we want you to be happy."

Nevaeh smiled gratefully at her friends. "I appreciate your concern, really. But for now, I'm comfortable continuing to hang out with Matt. We have a good time together, and if nothing else, we're friends. I promise I'll keep an eye out for any red flags, and if things change, I'll reevaluate."

Courtney nodded approvingly. "That's the spirit, Nevaeh. As long as you're aware of what you want and need, we're here to support you."

"You two got anything planned? A date or two? Hookups?" Mrs. Zhang purred like a cat while clawing the air with her fingers.

"You nosy woman!" Nevaeh exclaimed, her voice filled with a mix of surprise and amusement. Her friends scolded Mrs. Zhang in a light-hearted manner, teasing her. In the meantime, Rochelle arrived with their food, placing a platter of wings on the table. She cleared the empty tea tray that she had brought earlier. Nevaeh took a moment to compose herself, her hands tightening around her cup as she spoke. "Whenever we get to see each other, we always plan something, but as for what that might entail, I don't know," she said, puckering her lips playfully.

The women responded with a chorus of "ooo's," their voices filled with playful anticipation. Brandi playfully nudged Nevaeh three times, causing her to lean to the side and almost lose her balance and also reminding her of her aching shoulders. Nevaeh quickly sat back up once the commotion settled, and their conversation shifted to a different topic.

Brandi happily gave updates on her wedding arrangements when Mrs. Andrews requested details. Rochelle fit herself next to Nevaeh for this one, listening closely to Brandi's wholesome descriptions. "It's so much work, but I know it'll be worth it," Brandi said

"Aww, Brands, you truly deserve to have a fairytale wedding," Courtney sighed, resting her elbow on the table.

"I know," Joanne chimed in, her eyes glistening with emotion. It was evident that Brandi's happiness had a profound effect on her.

Nevaeh smiled softly, her voice filled with warmth. "You never know, Court. You just might be next. You and Justin have been going strong for a while now," she remarked, causing her friend to gasp in surprise.

"Oh, I would be the happiest girl if he got down on one knee. I have a feeling he might soon, but I don't know. I'm so nervous," Courtney admitted, her teeth clenched with a mixture of excitement and anxiety. The women reassured her, offering words of encouragement and support. Courtney shared the evidence that supported her hunch, and Brandi, in particular, affirmed her belief that the big question could pop up at any moment.

Nevaeh added her piece to this discussion by agreeing with Brandi, but was quietly reflecting. Would she ever be in Courtney's shoes, deciphering clues from her partner about a potential proposal? The idea seemed lovely, but she couldn't quite picture it with Matt. They enjoyed each other's company, but the thought of a future together hadn't crossed her mind. Did it mean she wasn't serious enough about relationships? And what did Matt think about their situation? Two years had passed since they started dating, if you could call it that, but their time together was scarce due to his frequent travels. Maybe their fondness could grow into something deeper when they were finally able to spend time together. She always felt she should be able to tell if she was with "the one" and she definitely didn't feel like that now, especially since she and Matt only had a casual relationship. She refused to have more with someone who was never there since he traveled so much. It was hard to imagine, but she had always dreamed of a happy marriage. Her friends were finding that happiness and she hoped it would come her way someday, too.

CHAPTER SEVEN

"And five, six, seven, eight..." Sean rhythmically snapped his fingers on each count, his body moving in sync with the vibrant music blaring from his phone. It was the dance-pop song that had caught the attention of the moms from Tia's school, and they had taken it upon themselves to learn the choreography. Together, they had mastered half of the routine, and Sean couldn't help but feel a swell of pride. Their dedication and enthusiasm were truly inspiring.

The women, filled with energy, began to freestyle as the song reached the portion where they hadn't learned the choreography. Sensing that time was slipping away, Sean quickly paused the music and pressed the power button on his phone. Instantly, the screen displayed the time, and he gulped, realizing they had gone over the scheduled class duration.

"All right, ladies, great class. We're making excellent progress," he said, moving away from the mirror to high-five each of them, while in the back of his mind, he could almost imagine Nevaeh's irritation at the delay. Punctuality had always been one of his strengths, but sometimes classes ran longer than intended, especially when students got caught up in their own excitement and distractions.

"Goodbye, Mr. Martin. Looking forward to next week," the woman with a red bandana and towel around her neck said as she gulped some water and exited the studio, waving cheerfully.

"You take care now," Sean gave a salute before whirling on his heel and running to the corner. There, he quenched his thirst with some water of his own before making a beeline for the door.

He jogged up to the front desk, a torrent of apologies ready to spill out. However, when he arrived, there was no sign of Nevaeh. His last student had just left, and apart from himself and Cynthia, the studio was deserted. "Huh? Did Nevaeh not come in today?" he asked his receptionist, feeling a pang in his heart. Whether or not he wanted to admit it, he had been eagerly anticipating his class with Nevaeh all day. She was his slowest student, and Sean secretly enjoyed witnessing the small progress she made with each lesson. Or so he told himself.

Cynthia lifted her eyes from her computer. "Nevaeh? Yeah, she did come about ten minutes ago. Why'd that class run so long? Did they pin you down in there?" She smirked playfully.

Sean playfully chided her, shaking his head. "Nah, nothing like that. They were just enjoying themselves," he replied. He scanned the small waiting room, hoping to spot his missing student as if she would magically appear. "Did she already leave? Where is she?" He spun on the heel of his ballroom shoes, trying to figure out where Nevaeh might have gone.

Cynthia cocked her head to the left. "You don't have to act so worried Sean. It's not like she's lost," she snickered. "Tia came out to greet her and explained you were busy. After that, she dragged her to your office for warm-ups."

"Oh," Sean croaked, embarrassment washing over him. "The office is kind of cramped but okay. Thanks," he replied, making his way down the hall toward his office.

He reached the office door and positioned himself behind the doorway, bending his neck forward to discreetly peep inside.

Inside, his desk was positioned against the back wall, cluttered with various items that had been hastily shoved there. Boxes of old files were stacked upon each other, creating a makeshift storage area. In the midst of the organized chaos, Tia took charge, providing instructions to Nevaeh on how to connect the dance moves they had been practicing.

"And ta-da! So don't stop in the middle. Just glide right in," Tia exclaimed, bouncing in place and clapping her hands with excitement. Her adorable face was filled with exhilaration. "You try. Come on!"

Nevaeh hesitated at first after Tia's countdown but eventually attempted the dance move on her own. However, her movements appeared more robotic compared to Tia's fluid motions. Sensing the need to intervene, Tia demonstrated "noodle arms" and encouraged Nevaeh to follow along.

"Now go crazy!" Tia exclaimed, wiggling her short arms with enthusiasm.

Nevaeh followed her with a laugh. "You must think I'm one of your little baby friends at school, huh?" She ended with a shimmy, leaning forward toward Tia.

Tia did the same, and they were soon shimmying together, having fun with it. In the end, they both giggled like old friends. Tia then held Nevaeh's hands and turned to face the door, audibly wondering whether Sean was ready. Suddenly, she caught him spying. "There you are!" Tia exclaimed, running to meet him with her hand still holding Nevaeh's.

"Don't drag me!" Nevaeh laughingly blurted as she hurried behind Tia. She used her arm to wipe sweat from her forehead. "Hey, Teach," she waved, pulling up the waist of her leggings. She wore a white crop top with black leather sleeves, and her hair had reverted back to its natural form, with curls braided down her upper back.

Sean's mood brightened, pleased to see her so upbeat. "Hey, I'm sure little T's been doing an awesome job getting you ready but now it's time for me to take over. T, finish up your homework while I instruct Nevaeh, okay?"

Tia resisted his directions. "I think I'll help you with Nevaeh this time. We had a good thing going before you came," she said, swinging her hand in Nevaeh's. "In fact, I'm probably better at teaching than you are," she added, poking a finger into her dimpled cheek.

Sean stood with arms akimbo, lifting his brows in surprise as he chuckled at her playful challenge. Meanwhile, Nevaeh watched in silence, looking like a snigger was threatening to unleash. He liked the look of her right now. Delight flattered her features. He could say that, right? It was merely a compliment. "Oh really? Well, I guess I'll have to step up my game then. How about we both teach Nevaeh today and see who she thinks is the better instructor?" he proposed, raising an eyebrow.

Tia's eyes lit up with excitement, and she nodded vigorously. "Deal!" she exclaimed, ready to showcase her teaching skills alongside her uncle.

Sean reconsidered, "I don't know. Remember, you got your final tests coming up. You can't afford to slack off., and then there's the homework you got," he challenged.

Tia did not let up. "I already *did* my homework. You know I finish fast. Plus, all my answers were correct; Nevaeh checked for me. And about the tests…" She tossed her braid off her shoulder. "We both know I'm on top of my work."

"Wow," Sean had to agree there. "Wait, so Nevaeh checked your homework?" he looked at the woman who'd been quietly digesting this exchange.

"Yup, I did. It's been a while since I've been in school, but Tia's level is something I can handle. She's like a math wiz. She solved every problem perfectly. Oh, her grammar was good too. You've got a little genius on your hands, Sean," Nevaeh gestured to Tia in amazement. She shared the child's confidence while nodding her head. "I think I'd learn a lot faster if she joined you in teaching. I mean, she's just got a way with instructing. Maybe it runs in the family?" she put the question to the cheeky little girl.

Sean was all ears for Tia's reply. Entertaining this might have been wrong in some parent manuals, but he saw his niece's defiance as self-expression. Her points were valid as well. Little Tia might make a great lawyer in the future. How proud he'd be if that happened.

"Nope. I think I'm just gifted. He had to read tons of books to get good at teaching while I'm good all on my own," Tia boasted, swaying from left to right.

Sean feigned offense while Nevaeh guffawed. She seemed to take heed of her loudness, and pulled her top over her lips. Her mild shame charmed him, as did the laugh. *Focus Sean,* "Well, guess I can't argue with facts," he held his chin in pensiveness. "Although, I do think I've got a little talent for teaching. Wouldn't you say, Nev? I mean, Nevaeh?" *Why did I shorten her name?*

Nevaeh showed no sign of having an issue with this. "I don't know Sean…" She stretched out his name and put a hand on Tia's head. "Whatever talent you *think* you have, Tia blows out of the water. I'm sorry, man, I don't make the rules." She clapped her hands gleefully when he exaggerated a gasp.

Sean placed his fingers on his chest in mock outrage, relishing the sweet laughter shared by his niece and student. Although he adored these playful moments, he maintained his role as the offended professional. "How dare you? I didn't teach for five years just to have the likes of you two make fun of me," he teased, but their laughter only intensified, causing them to double over and clutch their bellies.

"All right, you two, let's head to the studio," Sean declared, knowing that Tia's influence alone was enough to sway his decision. When it came to Tia, he was like a string tightly wrapped around her small finger, willingly yielding to her requests.

Toward the end of their session, Sean and Tia stepped aside, giving Nevaeh the floor to execute five steps in succession. With her eyes fixed on the mirrors, she displayed remarkable focus and determination. Sean and Tia clapped along to the rhythm, encouraging her every step of the way and reminding her to maintain proper form.

"Slide… snap, snap, and kick—oh!" Nevaeh's powerful kick propelled her body upward, causing her to lose balance. With quick reflexes, she managed to slide on her other foot and regain her stability, narrowly avoiding a fall.

Sean and Tia quickly rushed to Nevaeh's side, offering support and stability as she stumbled. Their voices filled with concern as they asked, "Are you okay? Are you hurt?"

"I'm good. Just great," Nevaeh replied, her frustration evident in her tone as she adjusted her clothing. She rubbed her tired eyes and sat down on the floor, crossing her legs to massage them. "How did I do, you two? Was I as bad as last time?" she asked breathlessly, giving them puppy eyes.

Sean became mush, almost failing to deliver an answer. "You… you were great. Still a bit awkward in some places, but your persistence is admirable." He joined her in sitting, hoping his words could soothe her growing insecurity.

"Yeah, my friend Angeline can't dance, and instead of trying like you, she gave up and said she couldn't do it. You're different, Nevaeh. You're a go-getter. My grandma says that's the best person to be." Tia sat beside her and offered a hug.

Nevaeh seemed to lose it, letting out a high-pitched 'aww.' "Tia, you're so cute. Even when you insult me." She playfully pinched the child's nose.

Sean appreciated when people showed affection towards Tia. He believed she needed plenty of it, and sometimes he worried that he might fall short in providing it. "Trust me, Nevaeh, she was being generous just now," he remarked with a smile, acknowledging Tia's kind gesture.

"Not just generous. I was nice. I said you're a go-getter." Tia punched Nevaeh's arm lightly, causing Nevaeh to whine and hold both of Tia's wrists as they continued to play around in a fit of laughter.

Sean watched them as they continued to bond, loving the light in Tia's eyes.

As Sean drove home, thoughts of Nevaeh consumed his mind. He couldn't help but dwell on the ease with which they connected and the natural chemistry between her and Tia. Their interaction resembled that of close siblings or a nurturing parent-child relationship. However, he quickly chastised himself for entertaining such thoughts. Nevaeh was his student, nothing more. Her friendliness and ability to connect with children were just admirable qualities that many people possessed. He had to remind himself not to read too much into it.

After dinner, Sean sat on the couch with Tia, carefully undoing her braids and gently brushing her hair. The television played cartoons in the background, a newfound interest since Tia had developed a liking for them. Tonight happened to be the premiere of a sequel to one of her favorite film franchises. The distraction of the show made it easier for Sean to complete the task of combing her hair. With practiced hands, he finished her cornrows effortlessly. She then prepared for bath time, ensuring she was clean and ready for bed.

Once Tia was dressed in her bow-themed pajamas, Sean allowed her to enjoy an hour of television before reminding her to brush her teeth before bed.

After reading her the story of her choice, he ensured that her flower-themed covers were neatly tucked under her body. Standing at the edge of her bed, he asked, "All set?"

Tia cuddled a fuzzy pink elephant, lying on her back with her satin bonnet covering her head. "Yup, all set and ready for sleeping," she said before sitting up suddenly. "Only that I'm not tired at all." Her gaze shifted to the small bookshelf against the opposite wall, its white paint matching her white-colored dresser. The drawer handles were pink, adding a touch of color.

Sean interjected, tapping her nose playfully as he sat back on the edge of her bed. "That's what you think. I'm willing to bet that if you lie down for just a minute, sleep will come flooding into your eyes." He then placed his hand on her chest, gently guiding her back to a lying position. "It's past your bedtime, so you should—."

"Nevaeh's really nice," Tia interrupted, with her head on her pillow.

"Nevaeh?" Tia's mention of her name caught him off guard, as thoughts of her had been occupying his mind all evening. "Yes, she is indeed very nice," he responded, acknowledging Tia's observation. "She's a great student, and her determination is truly astounding." He'd leave it at that. "Anyway, I should get ready for bed myself."

Tia's wide brown eyes locked onto his face. "She's pretty, too," she sighed longingly. "I wish we could be around her not just for class but all the time." Her long lashes batted with a pleading look in her eyes. "Why won't you make her your girlfriend, Uncle Sean? I know you like her. You always smile when she's there, and you think about her, too."

"Think about… What makes you think I think of this woman, T?" Sean chuckled nervously, feeling his palms grow sweaty. He knew Tia to be intuitive, but this was a bit of a stretch. "I keep saying she's just a student like the others. I know you enjoy playing with her, but that doesn't mean she has to be my partner."

Tia groaned, rolling her sparkly brown eyes. "Sometimes you just stand there and smile while looking at her. When you smile with Nevaeh, it's the same as your smile when you look at nothing and think about her. I'm seven, not an idiot," the child stated, her face falling into a somber expression.

Sean snorted, finding these mature expressions irresistible on that little face. This topic had overstayed its welcome, though. He thought Tia had moved on from it the last time they'd had this conversation. How was she so perceptive? It embarrassed him to think that he might have been obvious. "Look, Tia, when I think and smile, I'm thinking of you. You mean the world to me, okay? I don't need anything else in life because you're perfect."

Tia seemed less than impressed. "If you want a girlfriend, you can say it. It's not a crime to date, Uncle Sean. You *never* date. I thought it was just because you never met someone you liked, but now you've met someone and you won't even shoot your shot? Hopeless!" She wagged her tiny finger, tsking.

"What? Who says… Tia, it's time for bed, okay? You got school tomorrow, so snuggle up," he dried his sweaty palms on his pants, then rose. Sean lifted her bonnet past her forehead and kissed the little lady. Despite her resistance, he encouraged her to go to sleep. "You don't want to be sleepy at school," he hurried to the door and reached for the light switch.

Tia's eyes narrowed to slits. "You always do this when I talk about her."

"Are you ready for bed? I'm going to turn the lights off. If your eyes are open when the darkness hits, you'll have nightmares," he said, using the game as a diversion.

Tia gasped. "No!" She pulled her covers up to her face. "My eyes are closed. You can turn it off now," she mumbled from behind the sheet.

Sean felt accomplished after flipping the switch. "Night, T," he whispered before leaving her room and closing the door. Tia's intelligence never ceased to amaze him. At only seven years old, the child saw right through him. If she was like this now, he'd definitely have his hands full when she became a teenager.

He couldn't help but replay Tia's words about him and Nevaeh in his mind. "I don't have time for relationships," he muttered to himself. Relationships with students, in particular, were a no-no. So, as sweet, charming, endearing, and friendly as Nevaeh was, he simply could not allow any further development beyond their current dynamic. That being nothing, of course. Once she no longer attended his classes, he would move on. The thought weighed heavily on his spirits and tightened his chest.

CHAPTER EIGHT

"*I*t's been six weeks!" Nevaeh exclaimed, releasing her final pose and rushing towards her water bottle by the wall.

As she unscrewed the cap, she felt Sean's gaze on her through the mirror. He had wiped his chin with a towel. "Yes, it has, and you've made incredible progress toward perfecting these moves," he said, while Tia stood beside him, clapping enthusiastically.

Nevaeh ignored the heat on her face and took a long swig from her water bottle, consuming half of its contents. She slung her bag over one shoulder and approached Sean and Tia, who were waiting for her in the middle of the room. Sean's enthusiasm remained unwavering, and he continued to be a source of inspiration throughout her journey.

Nevaeh grew to appreciate him more with each lesson, admiring his gentle approach and patient instruction. In fact, no one else in her life came close to Sean in terms of kindness. Through their close interaction, she learned more than just dance moves from the mild-mannered man. His way of addressing her frustrations inadvertently taught her valuable lessons in patience and self-understanding. "I don't think it's *incredible* progress," she told him.

"It is for someone who started knowing nothing," Sean chirped, snapping his fingers to point them her way. Tia mimicked him and they struck the same corny pose.

Nevaeh couldn't help but feel a mix of appreciation and frustration toward Sean and Tia. In truth, she adored them both. Tia's recent assistance had made the lessons all the more enjoyable. With her hand lightly resting on her bag strap, Nevaeh walked over to Sean and the little girl. "I'm really grateful for your encouragement," she said, her gaze fixed on her sneakers. Maintaining eye contact was difficult, and she couldn't quite understand why.

Sean's warm hand gently settled on Nevaeh's shoulder, causing a faint shiver to course through her. As she lifted her gaze, she couldn't help but notice the tenderness in his eyes, and a subtle attraction stirred within her. His presence seemed to ease not only her anxiety but also awakened a newfound awareness.

"You're welcome. It's my pleasure. I wouldn't be a good teacher if I didn't support my students," he reassured her with sincerity.

The mention of 'teacher and student' abruptly killed her mood. "Right," she forced a smile and waved. "Anyway, I'll see you two. Tia, take care; and Sean, look after yourself, okay, Dancing Man?" With a brisk jog, she made her way to the door as they exchanged their farewells.

NEVAEH TURNED down the volume of her car radio while driving home from her dance class. She couldn't stop replaying the lesson in her mind. The steps on their own were not a problem for her, as she could perform them just fine. But putting them together smoothly seemed nearly impossible. Sean always emphasized the importance of practice, but she wasn't sure if it would really help. Doubts crept into her thoughts, and she questioned her progress. Despite Sean's unwavering belief in her, Nevaeh wondered if she would ever truly master the routine.

His 'teacher-student' statement kept resurfacing in her mind, gradually consuming her thoughts. The closeness they shared during their lessons, combined with his warm personality, led her mind to wander. Thoughts of him would sneak into her consciousness, sparking a sense of curiosity. It had been a couple of weeks since this peculiar interest had taken hold, coinciding with the time when Matt had once again let her down, causing her to close off any potential romantic thoughts about him. In the absence of Matt, her mind gravitated toward Sean, allowing her to entertain thoughts and feelings she had previously dismissed. She found herself wondering how Sean managed to maintain such unwavering positivity, which served as the catalyst for her growing interest in him.

He was a good-looking guy, no denying that. She had noticed it right from their very first lesson, though she hadn't really dwelled on it back then. Their interactions during that hour were enjoyable, but once Tia entered the picture, it changed things for her. It wasn't that she had anything against guys who were fathers, but the idea of dealing with potential complications or drama with the child's mother didn't appeal to her. Plus, it could mean that he was already taken. So, she made a conscious decision to keep her distance from Sean after that. However, lately, she found herself drawn to him again. And it didn't help that Tia was such an adorable kid. Nevaeh saw a bit of herself in Tia with her quick wit and confidence. Spending time with Tia felt like a fun party, and it reminded her of what people used to say about her when she was younger.

It must have been just last week when Nevaeh's curiosity got the better of her. She started digging, trying to uncover the story of how Sean ended up with a child and what happened to the mother. She searched for any clues or hints about her existence. So far, Nevaeh hadn't come across any signs of the mother, and from what she gathered through various sources, it seemed that there had indeed been a woman involved at some point. The mystery continued to intrigue her, and she couldn't help but wonder about the circumstances and the current status of their relationship.

As Nevaeh turned off her car's engine, she opened the door and let one foot dangle outside while keeping the other inside. She gazed at the apartment complex in front of her, noticing the warm glow of lights from the open doors. Across the way, she spotted a man chatting with a friend on a porch, enjoying a drink together. Her own place, a comforting haven, awaited her on the other side of the building. The clock in her car showed it was already late, around eight-thirty in the evening. The night sky twinkled with stars, but Nevaeh's mind was focused on the clues she had gathered, wondering what they could mean.

Rochelle mentioned a single woman who'd eaten at her diner with a toddler in the past. She'd come by once or twice but never became a regular. When she did visit, though, Rochelle would engage her in polite conversation, and based on what she'd gathered from their brief catch-ups, it didn't seem like a father fit anywhere in their picture. Rochelle's memories of Tia's mother dated years prior, but Nevaeh had taken note of this information for further consideration.

Rochelle's memories were a bit fuzzy, but they hinted that Sean and the woman with the toddler might have gone their separate ways. Nevaeh's initial assumption of a messy breakup started to fade as she gathered more information. She decided to ask a few coworkers who knew Sean from his dance studio about his relationship status. To her surprise, none of them had any knowledge of Sean being in a breakup or having a romantic partner. In fact, a couple of them mentioned that Sean didn't seem to be actively dating anyone. The more Nevaeh learned, the more it seemed like her earlier suspicions might have been off the mark.

Nevaeh would have disregarded the information if it hadn't been for Destiny, a recent high school graduate and intern, sharing what she had heard from some moms of Sweetgum Elementary School students. Surprisingly, Sean had become a topic of interest among the moms, with Destiny's eight-year-old sister overhearing their conversations at Sweetgum Elementary School.

The moms seemed to have an abundance of information about Sean, including details about his relationship status and his connection to Tia. According to Destiny's sister, the whispers indicated that Sean was single and had been since Tia was an infant. It was also said that Sean didn't have any children of his own, yet he played the role of Tia's parental figure, despite being her uncle.

With her door securely closed and locked, Nevaeh made her way toward the building, deep in thought. She couldn't help but question her reliance on alleged 'facts' provided by an eight-year-old, who was hardly a reliable source. Rochelle's investigation had yielded no significant information, leaving Nevaeh wondering why her older friend hadn't been able to uncover more about Tia's mother. The absence of any public encounters between the mother and Sean raised further questions. Nevaeh's instincts told her to dismiss the findings of the eight-year-old, but all the evidence seemed to suggest that Sean was a solitary figure. It was hard for her to believe that a man who showed little interest in forming intimate connections would end up with a child unless there was a tragedy or untold story behind it all.

Pausing with her hand on the door handle, Nevaeh took a moment to reflect on the pieces of information she had gathered. The sound of passing cars filled the street while the moon cast its gentle glow from above. Despite the fatigue from a long day of dancing and the ache in her body, Nevaeh's thoughts were firmly anchored to the ground. Inside her mind, she carefully laid out each puzzle piece and began connecting them, building a coherent picture. Rochelle's encounters with Tia's mother, Sean's apparent lack of a love life, the mysterious disappearance of the mother, and the rumors surrounding Sean's relationship to Tia as her uncle—all of it seemed jumbled and confusing, yet Nevaeh sensed that there was a story hidden within the chaos.

Nevaeh opened the glass door and briskly entered the lobby, offering a half-hearted greeting to anyone present. She quickened her pace and made her way to the elevator, the bright lights of the room catching her off guard after being outside in the darkness. As she pressed the button on the elevator panel, she crossed her arms and waited for the doors to close. "Tia's mom must be away for work, and Sean is taking care of her," she concluded, feeling a sense of satisfaction at solving the mystery. However, deep down, Nevaeh knew that her conclusion was far from the complete truth.

Her conclusion, though somewhat reassuring, left out a crucial piece of information—whether Sean was Tia's father or not. Despite asking various people and gathering tidbits of information, Nevaeh had failed to uncover the truth, as it appeared that Sean was a very private person. Among all her sources, Destiny's sister seemed to have the closest connection to Sean. Being a child who attended the same school as Tia, there was a possibility that this young informant held some valuable insights, even if they were in different classes. Nevaeh realized that she needed to dig deeper and perhaps engage in a direct conversation with Sean to unravel the mystery surrounding his relationship with Tia.

When the elevator dinged, Nevaeh entered the carpeted hall with a hand on her bag strap. Her digging meant one thing and one thing only. She'd lost her mind. Sean may have been sweet, patient, and handsome, but no man was worth losing her sanity. She bet once their lessons ended, he wouldn't give her a single thought. Yet here she was, shapeshifting into Sherlock Holmes over him. If only he could see her now. There was no way he'd invite her back.

I'm just curious, she thought. She flung her head back in a groan. It echoed against the ceiling, and she covered her lips, checking each door for angered neighbors. No sound could be heard from their dwellings. It appeared they'd settled in nicely for the night, leaving her as the sole resident hassling herself at this hour. "Fine," she sped-walked to her door at the end of the hall, vowing to leave these thoughts in the hallway.

They followed her to bed.

After applying her face mask and adjusting her bonnet, Nevaeh lay back, nestling into her pillow. In the darkness of her room, her thoughts went rampant. What if Sean really was married with a wife overseas? He wore no ring on his finger, but some men were sneaky. He might have hidden it. *No.* If Sean had a woman, he'd be loyal to her.

They'd only spoken to each other during and after classes, but she knew a good man when she saw one. This theory might explain why he'd never been caught with Sweetgum women, but the lack of a ring had her doubting. So far, the chances that his 'baby-momma' lived elsewhere seemed high, but that whole uncle scenario wouldn't leave her alone.

"Come to think of it," she said, with closing eyes. Her scented candle glowed warmly on her nightstand. Its aroma made her peaceful as she yawned on her words. "I've never heard Tia call him Dad." Had the child addressed him as 'uncle'? Nevaeh would have noticed that if it had happened. The two spoke like friends more than anything. Little Tia never called Sean by his first name but displayed comfort while with him.

She rolled to her shoulder with eyes half-open, leaning over to blow out her candle before settling back into her sheets. When Nevaeh had been little, she'd longed for a man to call 'daddy' in her life. At some point, her father had been there, before he'd decided he had better things to do than raise a family, but that was quite a long time ago. For so long, her mom functioned as her only guardian growing up. But boy, did she envy those girls who had fathers. *Daddy's girls.* She thought, foggy images of her own father filling her brain. Distant memories played out like a dream. She must have been a toddler in them.

As her father lifted her high and spun her around, she saw Tia's face where hers used to be. Soon, Sean replaced her hazy father and the two high-fived before sharing a handshake. She joined them and ended the fun by bumping her hip into Tia's. They'd already created several secret handshakes since meeting. How sweet was that? She thought of the spunky little girl; the child she saw herself in.

If they were anything alike, Tia wouldn't refrain from calling

Sean 'dad.' Nevaeh's gut told her that the child and Sean were blood-relatives, but… just not in the way she'd initially thought. *Destiny's sister was right.* Or perhaps Nevaeh wanted her to be.

Before sinking into sleep, she told herself to cut out the speculations. She saw Sean every week. It wouldn't hurt to ask directly. She just feared his perception of her. What if he found her nosey for inquiring? People asked questions of that nature all the time. She wasn't strange, was she? There was always the option of asking Tia herself, but that may present issues. Something seemed amiss with those two, but she didn't know what. Her safest bet was to present all questions to Sean. The six-year-old Tia needn't get involved. The weight of her day came crashing down and her sore body throbbed against her heavenly mattress. Its softness cushioned each aching muscle, leaving her completely relaxed when sleep finally took hold.

CHAPTER NINE

Every inch of this carving had been meticulously sculpted to perfection. Its surface felt smooth against Sean's palm as he held it in his hand. "Wow, this is incredible. Maybe when Courtney opens her gallery, you should consider showcasing some of your work there," Sean suggested, tracing circles on the wooden cup resting on Justin's table.

Justin shut his fridge with an elbow while holding two cans of soda. He set them on the table and sat beside Sean as the sound of cheering fans on his living room TV reached the kitchen. They made it a habit to meet up at least once every week, and more often than not, they would gather at Justin's place. While Justin didn't mind Tia being around if they met at Sean's, their intention for these meetings was to spend quality time together, just the two of them. That's why Sean left Tia with his parents, and Justin extended the invitation when Courtney had other plans.

"No. I wouldn't want to steal her glory. Not that my little old wood carvings are that impressive, but her gallery should be about her. All for her and what she does." Justin cracked open his soda and gulped down two sips. He raised the can to Sean, who clicked his against it.

Sean sipped his fizzy beverage, marveling at Justin's creative talent. "It's amazing how you found someone equally as artistic as yourself," he remarked, recalling the paintings he had seen displayed downstairs in the watch repair shop. He realized he hadn't complimented her work as much as she deserved. Some of her beautiful paintings adorned the walls of their living room, while the majority were neatly stacked in her and Justin's bedroom in preparation for her gallery. "If you and Courtney have children, they're bound to inherit the artistic genes. They'll be little Picassos," Sean commented with a grin.

"You're too generous," Justin said. "These are just little hobbies I indulge in when I'm bored or when inspiration strikes." He leaned back as if trying to catch a glimpse of the TV. "But Courtney, she's the true artist. Her talent is on a whole other level."

"No, both of you are. You two probably have a lot of fun when you organize date nights around paintings and carvings." Sean himself had suggested such ideas to Justin. Here he was, an expert at creating romantic scenarios yet having none of his own. As he envisioned his ideal date, the only woman who came to mind as a partner was Nevaeh. He sent the notion elsewhere to avoid complications. Going down that road would bring trouble. It didn't have to, but he always made excuses to stay far from romance. He was a parent before anything else.

"Mhmm," said Justin with his can between both hands. He brought it to his lips for a quick sip. "It's really a hoot and I sometimes wish they'd last forever." He seemed mesmerized by the droplets of water against his wooden table. "I want to be with her forever in general. Since she's moved in, life's been more incredible than I could ever hope." His words held conviction and earnestness. "Which is why I've been thinking of proposing," he faced Sean head-on, eyes determined.

It was a moment that Sean had anticipated, but hearing it now still caught him by surprise. A wide grin spread across his face as he leaned in for a heartfelt hug. Justin responded with a firm pat on Sean's back, the two friends sharing in the excitement.

"Man, this is incredible," Sean exclaimed. "Have you picked out a ring? Where is it? How long have you been planning this?" Engagements hadn't been something Sean often celebrated, but this was different. It was his best friend proposing, and it marked a new chapter after the heartbreak of Justin's first marriage. Courtney was everything Justin needed, and Sean couldn't be happier for them.

"For a while now, actually. I think she's kind of looking forward to it. I mean, we've been living together for months, and we know each other well. We spend every winking second of the day together and it's been perfect apart from a few hiccups over silly things, but that's normal people stuff." He inspected his carving, then stared right at Sean. "When I actually pop the question, I want it to be special."

Sean's heart swelled with happiness. "Yeah, it really does need to be. Courtney has brought so much joy into your life. I haven't seen you mope around since you met her," he remarked, taking a sip from his drink. The cold can left a slight moisture on his hands as he held onto it. "This is truly amazing," he continued, feeling grateful that his best friend was about to become a husband.

The love between Courtney and Justin was evident, and it was clear that they were both deeply committed to each other. Sean envisioned a future filled with happiness and love for them, and it brought him a sense of comfort. Courtney and Justin shared mutual feelings, and she loved Justin as Justin loved her, infinitely. Sean saw them living happily for years to come. How comforting it must be knowing they'd always have each other. He wished that—.

"Okay, you just said, 'this is amazing,' but now you look like you're brooding," Justin crushed his can after finishing the drink. "What? My proposal to Courtney feels out of the blue to you? I think this is just how it's supposed to work. Live happily together for a while, then bam! Proposal." He made jazz hands to accentuate his point. When Sean barely reacted, Justin furrowed his brows.

"Oh, wait, you're brooding over something else," he touched Sean's shoulder. "Are you thinking of…"

"No," Sean guaranteed that his silent reflection had nothing to do with his sister. "I was just imagining all the good times you and Courtney will continue to have here once you've sealed the deal, so to speak." He adjusted his chair so he was facing Justin. "I can't wait to see you spend the rest of your life with someone you love."

Justin arched one brow. "Okay? But that's not a bad thing. A moment ago, you looked doubtful. Or more… wistful? What?" his eyes widened. "You don't secretly like Courtney, do you?"

"Huh?" That was the last thing Sean expected to hear from him. "No way! Of course not. She's an incredible woman, but I haven't even spoken to her enough to catch feelings. What are you saying?" The random nature of this accusation was hilarious. "You have nothing to worry about."

Justin appeared to realize how strange his suspicion was. He patted Sean's shoulder as they both laughed softly. "So what is it, then? You scared she'll replace you?" he teased.

"No, Justin," Sean rolled his eyes in an exaggerated manner. "I guess part of me was just wondering if I'd ever experience what you have with Courtney. The intense bond, the intimacy. Don't get me wrong, I'm happy for you, but it was just a fleeting thought." He waved his hand in dismissal. "Let's not entertain it. I think you should consider getting her a really fancy ring." He wanted to support Justin however he could. "She strikes me as the type to love diamonds."

Justin shook his head. "I mean, yes. Courtney *is* a diamond girl, but I think that we've been overdue to talk about this for a while." He cleared his throat over the raging sports fans cheering in the living room. The signature hyperactive commentary from the commentators reached an all-time high as a player scored a goal. To them, this served as nothing but background noise, but to sports fans, it had to be a momentous occasion.

"Talk about what?" Sean cringed as he took another sip of soda.

As the years flew by and his taste changed, highly sweetened drinks and snacks became less and less appealing.

"Your love life, obviously," Justin cut him off before he could speak. "And don't give me that sorry excuse about Tia being your focus and how you have no time for women because of her and blah blah blah. Tons of single dads find time to date despite raising their children. Your personal life shouldn't suffer just because Tia is your focus. Look, right now, we're having a moment. If you want to date again, you can just drop her off at your parents' house like you're doing now. I understand that she needs attention, but you can organize things in a way that she gets enough while your life does, too." Justin had expressed this sentiment several times before. Whenever Sean heard it, his answer remained the same.

Sean pointed from Justin to himself. "Our guy's night is different than bringing some strange woman into her life. She knows where I am and who I'm with. If I were to date some random lady, it'd throw her off. She's young and still processing what happened to her mom." He redirected his gaze to the water on the table. "I don't know if I can do that to her. At least not yet," he murmured, seeing Nevaeh's smiling face. Why were thoughts of her constantly running through his head?

"I understand where you're coming from, but while you're exploring, I think it's important not to introduce her to the women you're meeting. You should only do so when you've met someone you're sure of. Just so she doesn't get confused." He looked at Sean with intensity. "But we've talked about this before, haven't we? How you'd do the whole dating thing if you ever got back on the market. It *is* possible, Sean. If you're truly interested." Another goal was announced, but the two men ignored it. "You are interested in someone, right? That's why we're discussing this?"

Sean thought of her mini tantrums and growls of agitation. He couldn't help but replay a particular instance where her hair hung in her face after she had danced with great effort. She made it look easy, being so gorgeous. "Yeah."

Justin paused, treating Sean like a test subject in the way that he scrutinized him. "So, there's someone you like?" he asked with caution, concealing a tiny smile threatening to take form.

Sean wanted to proclaim it right then and there, but it just struck him that Nevaeh and Courtney were friends. This posed no obstacles to his confession, but the realization caused a delay in his answer. "Remember my newest student?"

"The thirsty moms from Tia's school?"

"No, no," Sean's body went warm after memories of their class resurfaced. "Not them. I mean Courtney's friend. You know her. She gets mad easily when she doesn't catch onto moves and—"

"Nevaeh?" Justin's face lit up with realization. "Oh! You like Courtney's friend Nevaeh? That's amazing, Sean. Congrats!" He hit Sean's arm in a friendly manner. "How have the classes been going, though? Is she still on the first few moves?"

Sean liked how Justin addressed this; casually and easily. "Yes. She is, but we're getting there. She doesn't seem to think so, but I'm proud of how far she's come. It's hard for her to notice just how much work she's put in and the improvements she's made, but I do." He could dwell on Nevaeh as a subject all night but would hate to bore Justin. "I think she'll—."

"This is pretty incredible, Sean." Justin's brows went high as he tapped him again, this time more gleefully than earlier. "You like her. I would've never seen that coming, but I think you should go for it. Didn't you say that Tia likes her, too?" He was beaming with happiness.

"Yeah," Sean chuckled, reminiscing about the time he caught Tia and Nevaeh dancing to old-school Hip Hop in his office. They always found a way to have fun before Nevaeh's classes. They shared a special bond, but the thought of dating Nevaeh as his student gave him pause. "I'm just not sure if I'm ready to start dating yet. It's complicated, you know?" Opening up to Justin about his internal struggle felt comforting. After all, they had been best friends since kindergarten, and Justin always had a knack for offering valuable advice.

"If you ask me, the fact that you're interested in Nevaeh says that you *are* ready for dating. And I think, based on what we've said, that dating again will make you happy. Do you see what I'm saying?" Justin asked.

Sean gave it some thought. "I do, but…" he listened as a separate game began on the television. His TV back home only played cartoons and childish sitcoms. Overhearing sports matches reminded him of his days growing up when his father watched basketball and football at night. "Tia's so little."

"I know she is, but you're at your best when happiest," Justin said firmly. He hit the tip of his finger on the table. "And Tia deserves the best version of her parent. Won't dating make you happier? You looked so glad just now when we talked about Nevaeh." He drummed his fingers absent-mindedly.

"I looked glad?" Sean asked. His heart rate increased when Justin confirmed.

The other man continued providing advice. "Yeah, and the fact that you looked so glad means dating Nevaeh will make you happy," Justin surmised. "And like I said, you can only be your best self for Tia if you're happy." He leaned forward, locking eyes with Sean. "If that means dating Nevaeh, then you should go for it."

Sean nervously pinched the collar of his T-shirt, feeling the beads of sweat on his neck. "I mean, who said Nevaeh was the only person I'm interested in," he stammered, attempting to downplay his feelings. Despite his internal confirmation of his attraction to Nevaeh, the urge to deny it overpowered him. However, the words came out as obvious lies, and Justin's uncontrollable laughter only served to expose the truth.

"I think she is. And contrary to what you seem to believe, there's nothing wrong with dating your student." He appeared to reconsider this statement. "There's nothing wrong with dating your student when your student is around your age and is just taking temporary dance lessons until her friend's wedding."

The specificity of those conditions amused Sean. "Right. So only in that case can one date their student? That once in a lifetime scenario?" Sean poked fun at Justin's conclusion, to which Justin laughed. "Which also happens to be my situation?" He raised one eyebrow as Justin picked up Sean's abandoned can of soda. "You can have it, man. Knock yourself out."

"Nice. You can help yourself to some orange juice if you'd like. Just not the one in the transparent bottle. That's Courtney's," Justin informed.

Sean had already gotten up. He opened the stocked fridge and admired its organization. *Courtney's doing.* He held up a juice bottle for Justin's approval. "Convenient," he shut the door and leaned on the counter. "Okay, so you think I should date her?" his pulse raced like a track runner. The combination of enthusiasm and apprehension made him woozy.

"Do you want to?" Justin brought it back to Sean, challenging him to consider himself for once.

Sean exhaled deeply, his gaze fixated on the living room. His eyes settled on Justin's meticulously crafted rocking chair, becoming lost in thought. "Is she single?" he finally voiced his question.

Justin said nothing for all of ten seconds. He chewed his lower lip with eyes on the ceiling. "I actually have no clue."

"Are you kidding me?" Sean deflated as Justin apologized. "I thought Courtney always talked about her friends around you." He didn't mean to come off as mad, but it probably seemed that way. "I'm not angry, though. Just for the record."

Justin waved his hand dismissively, brushing off Sean's concern. "Don't worry about being angry, man. I should be the one who knows all this stuff," he said, squinting as he pondered. He rested his feet on Sean's empty seat, deep in thought. "Courtney has only mentioned Brandi and that girl from her book club when talking about people she knows in relationships. But I'm not sure about Nevaeh. Does she ever flirt with you? Is there a chance that she feels the same way?"

Sean imagined all the times she'd expressed gratitude for his patient teaching methods. She'd once called him 'the nicest guy' she knew, but that wasn't flirting. Although they did exchange compliments often. The first time was at their first lesson. "She told me I had a nice smile or something like that. Oh, once or twice she's said I was amazing, but that was just her liking my teaching style." He stabbed the sealed hole for the straw, then drank deeply. The cooling fruity beverage refreshed him. "I don't want to read too much into things."

"I think it could mean more, but let's leave that alone for now." Justin's chair legs scraped the white tiles when he turned them towards him. "Have you considered flat-out asking if she's single?"

Sean put his juice on the counter. "If she isn't and I ask, I'll make it obvious that I'm interested and ruin the mood of our lesson. A direct question can really destroy relationships. Our student-teacher dynamic would come apart, and she might find me creepy," he sighed in defeat, palm on his forehead. "Am I overcomplicating things?"

"No, I understand. It's hard when you like someone and aren't sure if they see you the same way. I'd thought it'd get easier into adulthood, but it's just as complex," Justin said reflectively. "If you show that you like her at your next lesson, it might let her know how you feel. And if she has someone, she'll let you down easy. To avoid awkwardness, you can say you weren't flirting."

Justin's idea felt silly to Sean. That and immature, like he was an anxious high schooler, avoiding communication for fear of rejection.

Justin appeared to observe his weariness. "Or I could just ask Courtney about Nevaeh's love life. There are perks to having your best friend date one of her best friends."

Sean scrunched his nose and scoffed disgustedly. "I'll handle this, okay? Like a man." As for what that meant? Sean didn't know. "I'll flirt more and see where it gets me."

"So, you're going with my first idea?"

Sean hadn't realized that his plan was the same as Justin's. "Oh yeah. I guess so, but if she catches on and there's someone else in her life, I won't act like a child and bail. I'd just say 'sorry' and move on. Hopefully, this plan won't blow up in my face."

"I'm sure it won't. Based on what you've told me, she might like you back. You need to stop doubting yourself." Justin stood. "Now, let's see what's on TV." He strolled to the living room and Sean followed.

Despite Sean's ongoing claps, Nevaeh found that they did little to improve her timing. She liked it better when Sean danced at her side. That way, she could mimic his moves by watching their reflection in the wall of mirrors. She tended to fumble when dancing alone since struggling to remember and execute the moves was difficult without a visual reference.

With each determined stomp, Nevaeh powered her way through the waltz, refusing to miss a single step. Sean, ever supportive, was ready to celebrate her completion of the dance, but she wasn't so quick to join in the festivities. She knew there was still room for improvement.

"One, two, three, and stop," Sean clapped, his voice brimming with genuine admiration. Shifting to her left, a warm smile illuminated his face. "You've really got it down, Nevaeh. Fantastic job! I'm thoroughly impressed." He fondly squeezed her right arm in encouragement.

Nevaeh's heart fluttered at the touch of his hand. Her mind went blank for a moment, lost in the sensation. "Well..." she managed to say, her voice slightly breathless as she regained her composure. "Don't patronize me, Sean! That was terrible. I was like an octopus out there," she complained, flailing her arms in frustration like an overstimulated child and consequently throwing off his hand. She couldn't focus while he was touching her. "Why do you keep telling me I'm good when it's clear that I'm not? I mean, I appreciate your kindness, but it's starting to sound a little crazy," she voiced her frustration. "I can barely navigate a waltz, and there are still dances I need to learn for Brandi's wedding," Nevaeh confessed, her anxiety growing as the wedding drew near and her progress remained stagnant. Taking a deep breath, she continued, "I'm scared, Sean. When I'm out there, I look like a wounded kangaroo."

Sean seemed to feel for her. "Wait, are you an octopus or a kangaroo?" He folded his arms on the question, showing genuine bafflement by her comparisons.

Nevaeh shoved him, but he didn't budge. Instead, he smiled, leaving her winded. Had she already mentioned how much she adored his winning grin? *Okay, calm down.* Matt had called last night, saying he was in town and wanted to meet with her and for her to give him a chance. She was conflicted. She needed to focus on resolving that situation before entertaining any curiosity about Sean. "I'm a mutated version of both."

Sean chuckled, shaking his head. "No, no, Nevaeh. You shouldn't say that about yourself. If you ask me, you're more like a gorgeous peacock, proudly displaying intricate patterns on its tail feathers." He casually licked his bottom lip after delivering the compliment.

Nevaeh was rendered speechless for an alarmingly long moment. Was he really doing what she thought he was? From the moment she entered the studio, he had greeted her with the phrase, "There's my favorite student," and throughout the hour, he had sprinkled in compliments about her form and execution that went beyond ordinary encouragement from a teacher. There was one particular comment he made about her pose that stood out, especially when he followed it up with a wink. Could it be possible that he was flirting with her? Was her interpretation correct?

"Aren't male peacocks the ones who show off their feathers?" she asked, a mischievous glint in her eyes.

Sean wore a face that expressed a mix of amusement and admission. "Touché," he conceded with a grin. "But hey, they all have those beautiful patterns, right? So maybe I'm not completely off the mark. Unless, of course, you find it strange to be compared to a bird," he teased, playfully nudging her shoulder. Nevaeh couldn't help but admire the pronounced arch of his jawline, a feature she had always found irresistible. The sight of it nearly made her weak in the knees, as she was a complete sucker for strong jawlines.

"No, no, I don't find it strange at all," Nevaeh replied, a playful glint in her eyes. "I actually enjoyed what you said. So, tell me more about these pretty feathers I'm supposedly boasting," she added, her finger absentmindedly twirling a strand of her twists. It had taken her four hours on the weekend to put them in, but she couldn't be happier with the result. Did Sean like her hairstyle? She believed so. She had caught him admiring it once or twice since they started their lessons. Perhaps he liked her in more ways than just as a student. But she had to remind herself of her meeting with Matt and the need to address their situation. Encouraging Sean's flirtation while still being involved with Matt didn't feel right. She had meant to end things between her and Matt, but she wasn't sure how to approach it. Although they were only casual, it didn't feel right to entertain the thought of Sean.

Sean looked downward, a hint of charm in his expression. "Believe me, I want to indulge in that topic, but we should try our hand at some other dance moves before you have to leave," he said, glancing at his wristwatch and then showing her the time. "We have about fifteen minutes left. How much do you think we can cover in that time?"

Nevaeh forgot they'd been dancing. "I don't know. We can try the cha-cha again," she dreaded this dance as she'd failed at it before. "Unless you'd prefer to *not* have your feet trampled by mine," she started to step but tripped on her lacings.

Like the hero he was, Sean swooped in to catch her. He held her upright, then retaught the moves she'd ruined. "It's not so hard when you get in the groove." Here he was, cranking up his optimism to support her like always.

For his sake, Nevaeh gave it another go, concentrating greatly on every motion. "Like that?"

"Incredible. Soon, you'll be teaching me. I'd be honored to have you as a teacher," Sean made conversation while they danced.

Nevaeh counted internally as Sean continued to sing her praises. "I'd be a terrible dance teacher. Talking and dancing at the same time messes up my rhythm. I can barely coordinate my own two left feet, let alone instruct others. You're just being kind," she said, though secretly enjoying his extravagant compliments. There was something endearing about his sweetness that melted her heart. If anyone else made such grand statements, she would have told them to tone it down, but with Sean, it was always appreciated. "But, if you want me to teach you, I can definitely give you a lesson in clumsiness," she said, smirking at him and meeting his gaze. Their eye contact momentarily broke her focus, causing her to pause. "Wait, hold on. Let me get back in the groove. Could you count down for me?" she requested, eager to regain her concentration.

Sean obliged and counted down for Nevaeh, helping her regain her focus. "I'd love to see it," he remarked, continuing to teach her some more choreography. She struggled to grasp the steps at first, but with his guidance, she gradually improved. As part of the routine, he spun her around gracefully and dipped her toward the floor, showcasing their synchronized movements.

"I'd love to sit through a lesson with you, and honestly, it doesn't matter what you teach me," Sean expressed, his voice filled with sincerity. He gently straightened her body, his touch sending a shiver down her spine. "As long as it's with you, I'll gladly listen and learn." His words lingered in the air, carrying a hint of something more than just dancing lessons.

Nevaeh's heart soared high like an eagle. "You're too great. Shut up." She playfully punched Sean's arm, and they both shared a brief moment of laughter. It felt different tonight; the atmosphere charged with a subtle shift. His kindness and flattery had always been there, but now it felt like he was trying to convey something more, sending a message she couldn't ignore. It would be foolish of her not to receive it, to not explore what could potentially blossom between them.

But her plans with someone else stood in the way, causing Nevaeh to resist Sean's advancements for now. "Okay, what's next?" She consciously shifted the conversation, feeling a pang of discomfort as she redirected their focus.

There was a memo that Sean needed to receive—they could revisit their connection once she resolved things with Matt. After all, Matt had made a significant effort to come all the way from across the country to meet her, and it wouldn't be fair to abruptly end things on their date. Besides, Nevaeh couldn't be certain if Sean's flirtatious behavior was genuine or simply a friendly gesture. Despite her internal struggle, she couldn't deny her growing attraction toward him, and any small indication that he might feel the same way stood out amidst her uncertain thoughts.

He pleasantly suggested they start on the Samba, and Nevaeh readily agreed. As the session came to an end, a bittersweet feeling washed over her. Despite her fumbles and mistakes, she had genuinely enjoyed herself. Being in Sean's presence always brought her a sense of tranquility. For that hour, all her worries and troubles seemed to fade away as she followed his lead on the dance floor. Dancing may have been a challenge for her, but with Sean as her partner, it felt like stepping into a beautiful dream. His quick reflexes and support were always there when she needed them, making her trust him without hesitation. The thought of remaining close to him within the confines of that dance studio felt enchanting, as if it were a world meant only for the two of them.

"Well, I better head off," Nevaeh said, her voice laced with a hint of reluctance. She took a sip from her water bottle by the door, purposefully elongating her actions, almost as if she hoped that Sean would intervene and ask her to stay.

Sean finished his stretches by the wall near the windows, and as Nevaeh prepared to leave, he raised his hand in a farewell gesture. "Remember, if you ever get the chance, it wouldn't hurt to review what we practiced. There are plenty of resources online to help you as well," he suggested. "But don't become too skilled without me. I want to be there for every step of your dance journey. You're... an exceptional student."

Nevaeh felt a surge of emotions, her heart fluttering at Sean's words. How else could she interpret being called an "exceptional student?" It went beyond her dance skills; it felt like a personal compliment. He liked her, and instead of seizing the opportunity, she had simply walked out of his studio, exchanging a half-hearted laugh and waving goodbye. What a missed opportunity it was. If he have asked her out, would she have said yes? It felt wrong to reject him after the enjoyable banter they had shared. But the class had come to an end, and she found herself on her way to the exit, bound for her date with Matt. Realizing she only had an hour to prepare, Nevaeh hurriedly made her way to the parking lot, her mind consumed by thoughts of what could have been.

A WARM, rosemary-scented candle flickered on Nevaeh's kitchen counter, creating a cozy ambiance as she prepared for the evening. While she occasionally enjoyed cooking her own meals, her busy schedule often led her to opt for the convenience of takeout. On nights like this, after her classes, she found solace in Mrs. Zhang's delectable spicy noodles. They were a true lifesaver. Today, she had picked up two servings of the noodles on her way home, knowing that Matt had expressed his love for Chinese cuisine. She believed he would appreciate the gesture. Besides, whether the food was freshly cooked or takeout didn't matter to him. His voracious appetite ensured that he relished every bite. She still remembered how she had giggled the first time he declared, "As long as it's good, I'll eat it."

"Mmm," Matt said, his locs hanging over the bowl as he skillfully twirled the noodles around his chopsticks. He wiped away a stray droplet of soup from his chin with a loose napkin. "Anyway, so that's what happened with that," he continued, his eyes focused on Nevaeh as he recounted his day.

Nevaeh noticed the new ear-piercings he had gotten since their last meeting. He always took pride in his appearance, and today was no exception. He was dressed in a sleek outfit, sporting a collared denim jacket layered over a white tank top. The jacket and jeans gave off a grungy vibe, but he had added a touch of semi-formal flair with his recently released dress shoes from a well-known brand. A stylish brown belt with a flashy buckle cinched his waist, completing the ensemble.

She admired how well-groomed he looked, from his neatly trimmed beard to his perfectly shaped eyebrows. His locs were styled in a trendy half-up, half-down hairdo, with two strands falling gracefully on his forehead, adorned with gold bands. Matt always paid attention to the details when it came to his appearance, and it certainly didn't go unnoticed by Nevaeh.

Nevaeh took a hearty bite of her noodles, savoring the flavors before speaking. After she had swallowed and patted her napkin against her lips, she asked, "Sounds like a nightmare. Did you guys end up canceling the show? I can't imagine anyone sticking around after a flood ruined the venue."

She had taken the time to shower and dress up for the evening, opting for a black halter dress she had carefully chosen earlier in the day. The skirt of the dress fell just above her knees, elegantly spreading out like a blooming flower. Nevaeh had expected Matt to notice and compliment her on her appearance, but he hadn't said a word about it since entering. They had exchanged a hug and a chaste kiss, and then he had enthusiastically shared details about his new shoes. Now they were comfortably seated at the table, engaging in conversation.

Matt took a sip of his soup straight from the bowl, displaying his casual and laid-back demeanor. "Yeah, we had to cancel, but even the greatest DJs and musicians have to cancel a show once in a while," he reassured her, trying to alleviate any concerns. "The date got postponed, so next time I'm away, I'll have to make up for it." He idly played with his chopsticks, pinching them together as he spoke. "So, what's been new with you? We barely get a chance to talk these days."

Nevaeh skillfully secured a chunk of chicken between her chopsticks, appreciating the delicious flavor before responding. Although frustrating, she understood the challenges of their busy schedules and the complications caused by different time zones. "Yeah, it's true. You're always busy, and the time difference can make things tricky," she acknowledged, giving him a small smile. She had decided to be understanding about his previous cancellation, knowing that being a musician came with its own set of demands and unpredictable situations.

"As for me, things have been all right," she continued, taking a moment to collect her thoughts. "Work isn't too demanding, and my friends are doing well." She took a sip of her drink, pausing for a brief moment. "But the one thing that has changed is that I've started taking dance lessons," she proudly shared, wanting to captivate his interest.

Her lack of dancing skills had been a running joke between her and Matt. She worried that their conversations might become monotonous for him, considering his exciting life as a traveling musician. Sweetgum, their small hometown, lacked the thrill and excitement he was accustomed to. However, tonight she had something different to share, something that would pique his curiosity. She anticipated the questions that would inevitably follow her revelation.

"Really?" Matt raised an eyebrow, his wine glass held elegantly in his hand. Nevaeh had carefully selected a bottle of red wine, now sitting at the center of her rectangular table. Normally left bare, tonight, she had adorned it with a flowing red tablecloth, adding a touch of sophistication to the ambiance.

"Yup. I have to say that it—"

"That's cool. Oh, you know, that reminds me of something!" Whatever he thought of seemed to excite him. He sat upright, eyes widening. "Remember, James?"

Nevaeh's joy took a sudden nosedive, causing the corners of her lips to droop. Despite the disappointment, she fought to maintain a composed expression. "The keyboard expert?" she murmured, absentmindedly tracing circles around the rim of her glass. She decided to hold back her news until after he finished his story, giving him space to share the details.

"Yes. He started dancing recently too. There's this awesome instructor over at—"

"We have a great instructor here at Sweetgum, actually. Have you ever heard of a Sean Martin?" Nevaeh interjected. Now he had to realize that she wanted his attention.

Matt quieted down. "Uh… no, actually. He's your teacher?"

Finally. "Yes. And he's been amazing with me. I haven't really mastered anything, but I can follow the steps of a waltz. Want me to show you?" *Actually, it might be better if I didn't.* "Never mind. You can see it at Brandi's wedding. She wants me to dance there. It's why I'm having classes in the first place." He looked rather attentive. She knew this would interest him.

"Ah, okay. That's nice. Can't wait for the wedding." Matt threw two pieces of chicken in his mouth. He swallowed them so fast that Nevaeh feared he hadn't chewed. "James' instructor calls himself 'The Mood,' and boy, is he a mood. He's like—" he went on to give a long-winded explanation on how this 'The Mood' person assisted his friend. After that, he told her all about what he'd learned from him. One thing led to another, and he wound up describing a show he'd danced at. From there, he talked about other shows too, and their difference in venues.

Nevaeh got a word in sometimes, but mostly, Matt dominated their conversation. He'd had quite the eventful trip, so she could not blame him. It still hurt, though. After being the center of Sean's world at his studio, her supposed man had relegated her to an afterthought.

CHAPTER ELEVEN

Once again, Sean found himself watching Nevaeh struggle through the dance moves. He had gone over each step with her multiple times, and he believed that she was ready to tackle them on their fifth attempt. But he quickly realized how wrong he was. As the music played from his phone's speaker, Nevaeh slid, tripped, and stumbled over her own feet. Sean offered to turn off the music, sensing her frustration, but she vehemently resisted. It seemed like she was determined to battle through the choreography, even though she kept hitting the same wall every time. It was a shame, though, as the song was already halfway through, and the dance had been choreographed specifically for the chorus.

But that meant nothing to the incandescent beauty. She yelled at herself whenever she fumbled and screamed when she stepped out of time. As her teacher, he had to intervene as the activity entered toxic territory. He went for his phone, which was lying on the floor, determined to put an end to the ordeal. "I'm turning it off," he declared firmly, his voice cutting through the chaos of the music.

"No, I said don't do that. How will I learn on my own if you're this lenient?" Nevaeh ran on her bare feet to stop him.

Though Nevaeh was closer, Sean reached the device first. He

paused the song, then hid his phone behind him. "Nevaeh, your self-talk is horrible." The room's newfound silence made space for her huffing. Her twists, which were neat when she'd first come in, were now fuzzy from all her angered tugging. It hurt seeing her worked up, but something about it endeared him. But as usual, he wouldn't dare reveal this.

Nevaeh used her collar to wipe her face, and sweat soaked her blouse. Her hoodie was no longer on her shoulders. She'd wrapped its arms around her waist to ward off the heat. Under his radiant studio lights, the sweat on her legs seemed glossy. She had never looked so gorgeous. He inhaled her fading perfume after narrowing the gap between their bodies.

"How can it not be when I've been seeing you for so long and still can't dance? I'm wasting Brandi's money!" Nevaeh cried in panic. She slapped her forehead and paced in small circles. "Why can't I dance? I have a good teacher; I'm putting in the work, I—" As she went on, the open back windows allowed cool air to drift in.

Sean heard rolling wheels and engines outside. The room had grown stuffy from non-stop dancing. When the air hit his face, it connected him to the rest of the world, subduing his tension amidst his worry for Nevaeh. Was that what she needed? A refresher? They'd been at it for a while, hadn't they? "Okay, okay, look." He put his hands on her shoulders, telling her to breathe.

Nevaeh moaned and refused his instruction. "I can't breathe right now, Sean. You need to reteach me that part. The one that I keep messing up in this stupid Samba." She stomped her feet before demonstrating. "This part right here. When it's time to do the thing I can't do it." Her failure to articulate her thoughts proved all the more that she was due for a break. A sound mind aids productivity. Sean taught young children; he'd seen how restlessness affected learning. Heated emotions were a stumbling block to reception. Nevaeh knew the steps, but was too agitated to deliver them.

As tears welled up in Nevaeh's eyes and she continued to babble in distress, Sean gently placed his finger on his lips, shushing her with the tender gesture. At first, she didn't respond to his efforts, but gradually, she began to unwind, exhaling a sigh of defeat. In the ensuing silence, he took her hand and guided her towards the window.

"What are you doing?" Nevaeh whined as they faced the glass. Sean opened the window wider, allowing a refreshing breeze to enter the room. Instantly, Nevaeh's demeanor changed. The furrow between her brows disappeared as her hair danced in the wind.

"We don't often get such pleasant summer breezes, do we?" Sean remarked as a jeep drove by, the sunlight still lingering despite the late hour. A few stars shimmered in the orangish sky as night slowly encroached on the fading daylight. As he took in the beauty of the scenery and the surrounding buildings, he could sense that Nevaeh was captivated by the same view. The passing vehicles, in particular, held her attention, moving in a rhythmic pattern before changing direction and disappearing from sight.

Nevaeh finally swallowed a large gulp of air. "Okay, Mr. Zen. I'm calm now. Can we continue?" she held down her head and crossed one leg behind the other.

Sean couldn't help but find Nevaeh's pout endearing, though he didn't want to encourage it further. "Why the long face?" he teased, gently tapping her chin.

Nevaeh's head jerked up in surprise as his finger made contact, and for a moment, Sean worried that he had crossed a line. They had been in physical contact during their dance lessons, but he had consciously tried to avoid any unnecessary touching outside of those sessions. Had he unintentionally gone too far? Flirting was one thing, but getting physically intimate, even in the smallest ways, could complicate their relationship. He hadn't considered that aspect until now. It had simply felt natural to…

"My face isn't long," Nevaeh retorted with a playful smile, tilting her head to the side and putting her finger between her teeth, acting like an adorable, smitten child. "See?" she dropped the act and grinned openly.

A wave of relief washed over Sean. She wasn't offended. "Well, alrighty then. Let's get back to it," he said, quickly moving to the mirrors, and Nevaeh walked alongside him. He was ready to dive right back into the routine, but he could still sense a lingering tension. "But first," he reached into his pocket and retrieved his phone.

Nevaeh groaned in mock exasperation. "What now? Are we going to meditate? Sean, this is a dance class, not a temple," she playfully teased, taking the initiative to go over the choreography. "Look, am I doing it right?"

"You are, but don't you want to go crazy for a little?" He showed her his playlist of popular hits.

Nevaeh swiped down the long line of tunes. "Woah," she hit him on the back after grinning. "You never told me you had good taste. Look at these. All my favorite artists are in here. Sean!" She hopped around with a squeal. "You like music?"

She packed a mean hit. The sting sizzled his spine even now, prompting him to scratch it. "Yes. Why wouldn't I? Dancing and music go hand in hand, don't they? You can't dance without music." He took back his phone and tapped the first song. The distinct bassline had him bobbing before the beat and treble swooped in. He put down his cell and started to gyrate.

Nevaeh's mouth hung open and she blinked repeatedly. "Sean!" she raised a finger at his waist. "Look at you!"

Sean spun around then posed. "That's how I dance when no one's around." He held out a hand. "Care to join me? Doesn't matter what you do, as long as you have fun. Let's go. You know this one." He pulled her forward, then released her to snap his fingers. "Come on, Nevaeh. Show me what you got." She laughed and swayed and his heart skipped a beat. Nevaeh profoundly affected him; if she smiled too widely, he just might faint. Her coy shimmies weakened his knees.

Nevaeh gracelessly kicked her legs around and leaned back with arms flailing. She alternated between jumping from one foot to the other then raised both hands. Her twists flipped when she whipped her head from left to right. "Getting scared yet, Sean?" she asked with hips jerking. "This is how I dance on a night out when the lights are extra dim." She slid forward until they breathed on each other. "Emphasis on the extra dim."

He laughed, but not at her. She'd been so insecure about her dancing on their first encounter, but now she could joke about it. "I love it. And I love that you're no longer ashamed of how you move. Right now, it's all about letting loose. Let me see you spin." He twirled like an expert.

Nevaeh jumped and whirled her body while airborne. She landed unsteadily, as he expected, and he held her upright. They shared a laugh, and she danced a while longer. "And by the way, I'm still pretty embarrassed about this, but since it's just you and me and we're having fun, it's okay to get crazy." She clapped and tromped childishly.

"So, this is exclusive?" he asked, his heart rate increasing at the prospect.

Nevaeh punched at the ceiling and rocked her hips. "Yes. Just an 'us' thing. You aren't expecting more students to barge into this place, right?" She went rigid with anxiety checking the door for what she feared.

With fire burning in him, he stretched for her face. Gently, he held it and steered it towards his. In her eyes was delighted stun and a soft warmness. He let go with his heart pounding mercilessly. "You're my last student," he told her. "Now come on, this next song is a classic."

Nevaeh took a while, but eventually returned to the moment. "Ooh. You're so right. Let's do this Nevaeh-style," she squatted and rolled her upper body like a worm. After coaxing Sean to do the same, he gladly obliged.

They goofed off to one more song before Sean called 'time' on their recess. There was still a lot to cover. As he paused the music, Nevaeh quenched her thirst while she sat on the floor. With her legs crossed and water on her chin, she swallowed large gulps. "So, we're ready?"

"Yeah. Just ten more minutes to go, but I need to reteach you that step before you try by yourself one more time." He massaged a few knots in his arms, then took a stance. "You can take another five if you'd like, though. You've been on your feet for an hour." He revisited the choreography and performed it with ease. "Takes focus and practice," Nevaeh's reflection stood behind his while he counted from five.

"I didn't see Tia when I came in today. How is she?"

Sean ended his demonstration and met her eyes in the mirror. "She's good. Sorry for being so early to class. You didn't get to chat with her before we started." He pictured all the times he'd caught them catching up when his previous class ran long. Tia talked about Nevaeh at home every day. His niece admired Nevaeh's drive and self-assertion, good qualities to look up to. He, too, adored these qualities in his student and applauded Tia for choosing her as a role model. It helped that Nevaeh looked amazing, but Sean tried to enforce the view that one's personal qualities were worth more than appearances.

Nevaeh tucked her twists behind her ear. "No, it's okay. I'll check in with her before I leave." Her tonal quality turned the mood somber. She cast her eyes on the floor as her mouth twitched slightly. "So, um… she's yours, right? Your daughter?"

He digested her question and gave thought to his answer. "Um… well, yes and no. I mean—" Distant memories of a time he forgot stole his breath and tugged at his heartstrings. He abandoned their reflection to stare her in the face. "I see her as my own and we are blood relatives, but I'm actually her uncle."

"Oh," she blinked in enlightenment, then tilted her head. "So…"

"I know. You're wondering what happened to her parents." Sean couldn't look at her anymore.

"If it's a touchy topic, then you don't have to tell me."

"No, no, you should know. You're someone she looks up to and a person I've come to admire." He put on a smile which Nevaeh returned. His smile fell as he thought back to that time period. "You see, I moved back to Sweetgum after college because my sister had Tia."

"Sister?" she whispered.

"Yeah, we were twins," he said. "Tia's dad was never in the picture and never turned up, so I decided to help. Of course, our parents helped too, but I was the main one assisting," he recalled those tiny hands gripping his fingers. Baby Tia had been a sight to behold. The most perfect living being to ever surface. Her beauty evolved along with her. That child was an angel incarnate. "It was fun though, we had our challenges, and I look back at that time fondly." His voice hitched as he started to continue. "But the good times didn't last." His legs wobbled for another reason entirely.

"You should sit. Come on. Let's sit," Nevaeh rubbed his arms, then helped him to the floor. He did so absentmindedly, reliving that earth-shattering experience all over again. It'd been long enough that he no longer wept at the recollections, but they still hurt. Like a bone broken but never set straight.

"When Tia was only two years old, I found my sister unresponsive in her apartment. I'd gone to pick up some groceries while she watched T and... it happened so suddenly." He zoned out and heard the distant echo of his wailing beside her dead body. "An aneurysm. I guess she was more stressed than she led on." He slid his hand down his face. "We'd all been devastated, but the big questions needed to be answered. Who would raise Tia? She was only two and needed a parent figure more than ever at that stage." He told himself he wouldn't cry, but the tears were relentless. Quickly, he swiped two away and checked on Nevaeh.

Her eyes were just as wet as his. A tear spilled down her cheek, but she let it fall smoothly. "So, you volunteered," she finished on his behalf.

"Yeah. My parents were older and had raised two children already. They'd also made plans to travel for retirement, so I just... I couldn't expect them to do this. Don't get me wrong, we all love Tia, but they were in no place to raise a little child."

"I understand what you mean," Nevaeh comforted.

"Right," he heard the compassion in the cracks of her pitch. "So that was why I stepped up and took her in. Ever since then, I've been the only father she's known. Try as I might, I couldn't contact her biological dad after my sister's sudden death, so I had to be there. His name isn't even on Tia's birth certificate." Now that he finished the story, a certain lightness came over him. Justin was the only person who knew his and Tia's full story, apart from his parents. Other people in town had picked up after watching the events unfold, but he hadn't sat and talked about this with anyone.

Nevaeh's hand gently brushed against Sean's on his lap, their fingers seamlessly intertwining. In her eyes, a glimmer of emotion welled up, accompanied by a trembling smile. She expressed her gratitude with heartfelt sincerity. "Thank you for sharing."

Sean squeezed her fingers. He wanted to thank her for lending a listening ear and to admit that it helped him.

"Boo!" Tia's enthusiastic shout filled the studio as she burst in.

Normally unfazed by such predictable pranks, Sean found himself caught off guard after opening up to Nevaeh. Startled, he jolted, his free hand instinctively clutching his chest.

Her expression mirroring Sean's surprise, Nevaeh let out a distressed whine. "Tia," she protested. "Your uncle and I were having a moment." She gently soothed Sean's knuckles with her thumb, a gesture of comfort.

Tia spun and skipped to her heart's content. "Yay! For the first time, I scared Uncle Sean!" She swung her little hips and pumped her arms in and out victoriously. "I always scare you when I try Nevaeh, so it's not such a big deal, but Uncle Sean? I will write this down to remember forever!" She ran up to them and sat in front of the two.

To see her so full of life after reliving their hardships swelled his heart unfathomably. He listened to Nevaeh's delighted laughter, then planted a sloppy kiss on Tia's cheek. "You got me."

"Uncle Sean!"

The adults doted on her while she made her complaints. Tia truly was a gift. Even if she didn't see herself as Sean did. He could tell that Nevaeh shared his opinion. *Thank you,* he thought in awe of her presence. *I needed that.*

CHAPTER TWELVE

$\mathcal{N}$evaeh frequently thought about Sean over the next few days, which was understandable after all he'd shared with her. Throughout her prior snooping, she'd figured that a tragedy might have been at play for Tia to wind up in Sean's custody, but hearing it directly from him ruined her. Sean's determination to be there for Tia after losing her mom was beautiful, but it didn't change the devastating events that led to their situation. Nevaeh couldn't imagine how lost he must have felt after finding his sister unresponsive that day. And to deal with taking care of a child on top of his grief? Most men, no, most *people*, would have backed down. But not Sean. What a warrior.

She greeted Cynthia at the front desk after arriving at her lesson fifteen minutes early. Normally, she'd go find Tia to practice with her before going into the studio, but she preferred to reflect quietly this evening. All this dancing had her muscles sore. Her physique was well toned, but it came with a price. She deserved to use the time to just sit and wait.

Nevaeh sat across from the front desk. She put her arms on the armrests and leaned her head against the wall. Vibrations from sound waves in the other room coursed through her body. A familiar song rang out and sedated her as she welcomed the vibrations.

She would have fallen asleep if her phone hadn't rung. Nevaeh sat forward, then took out her cell, reading the ID. It was Matt. They'd caught up again since their date at her place but not through any formal means. Just random texts. He hardly called unless something major arose.

"Hello?" She walked over to the doorway and leaned her back against it. The atmosphere's warmth caused sweat to rise on her cheeks. Again, the sun shone brightly, ignoring the evening hour.

"Hey, Nevaeh, what's up?" She heard his hurried footsteps and rushed breathing through the line. "Listen, I have to hit the road sooner than anticipated. We just got a few surprise-gigs this week across the country so I'm heading back. Just thought you should know."

He usually stayed in town much longer. This news was disappointing, especially with the wedding coming up. "Gigs? But…" she saw Cynthia avert her eyes from her face. Sean and she talked often. Could she tell that Nevaeh was speaking to another man right now? Would she tell Sean? Nevaeh had no time to deliberate this. "What about the wedding?" She stepped outside for more privacy, watching as birds flew past thick poofy clouds.

"Don't worry. I'll be back in time for that. Nothing to fret over, okay?"

Nevaeh screwed up her mouth at how flippantly he said this. "Okay, well—"

"I have to go now. Bye!" Matt hung up without warning and she covered her face.

"Yeah, bye." Nevaeh dropped the hand with her phone in it, then sighed so heavily it might have left her weightless. He would be back, right? He always came back. Duty called time and time again, but Matt never failed to return. Hopefully, nothing else would pop up to steal him on the day of Brandi's wedding.

"Why are you out here all by yourself?"

Nevaeh got tingles all over when Sean's question reached her ears. She took in his signature dance attire accompanied by the genuine elation lighting up his face. "Sean," she looked at her phone screen and thought of Matt. The other man Sean knew nothing of.

His last students left the building at that point, prompting her to give them room by stepping to her left. Sean had opened up to her last week and yet she hid this from him. What would he say if she told him? It wasn't like she and Matt were serious. But she supposed that counted for something, since she hadn't cut ties with him like she'd wanted.

"Shall we?" Sean directed an arm to his studio to grab her attention.

Nevaeh left her trance of guilty reflection. "We shall." She followed him in with her stomach in knots.

Shaking off her shame was impossible. It consumed all aspects of her mind and kept her distracted during their lesson. Sean showed no sign of irritation when she requested he repeat himself, but his patience only agitated her guilt.

He was just this kind, sweet man she felt she was leading on while having someone else in the picture. Even though he never said anything outright, she picked up his clues and she reciprocated. If she were in Sean's position, if she found out the truth on her own, she'd ban her from the studio. *That's a bit harsh but he's shown me nothing but care and honesty.* The betrayal would leave a lasting impression. *But Matt and I aren't—*

"Careful!" Sean stretched out a hand when she spun into the mirror.

Nevaeh knocked not only her hip and shoulder but also her skull upon the cold glass. For a second, she feared that she'd broken it, but after dropping to her rear, she took solace in finding the glass intact. "Thank goodness," she crushed the fabric of her blouse near her breast, then hung her head. Though she hadn't cracked it, she did leave fog and sweat streaked across its surface. Normally, the embarrassment would kill her, but she was too preoccupied to care.

With her head bowed in misery, she suddenly saw Sean's extended hand. Though it hurt to do so, she accepted his help and got to her feet. "Sorry." Her eyes stayed on the freshly waxed floor as opposed to his eyes of compassion.

"It's okay. Mistakes happen but… today you seem a little off," he said.

"What do you mean? I'm the worst dancer on the planet. I'm always off." A scenario played in her head where Cynthia laid everything out to Sean after Nevaeh's departure. In her tortured mind, Cynthia used nasty terms to label her, to which Sean agreed. *Giving him signs when there's someone else.*

Her relationship with his niece would come up, too. How Nevaeh involved the poor little girl when her intent was to break the heart of her uncle. In Nevaeh's mind, Cynthia put it in the worst way possible to turn Sean off.

"No, no. That's not true." He held her cheeks, causing her to look at him. "I know my students. Nevaeh, you're always attentive and asking how you can improve. Even if you don't get the steps right away, you keep your head and practice until you get it. That's the Nevaeh I've come to know." He put his hands behind him. "But this Nevaeh is carrying a weight. So much that it's crippling." His dark brown eyes searched hers for more details. "Is everything okay?"

Telling him was suicide, but what other option did she have? She needed to stop considering her own selfish desires and open up to this man. "There's this guy who comes to Sweetgum whenever he's not working out of state and when he does, I usually spend time with him!" she cried out.

Nevaeh shielded her face with an elbow, protecting herself from the wrath that lay dormant behind Sean's benevolence. "There I said it. I—I should go, right? I'm sorry Sean, you're so amazing and I do want to explore whatever this is, but I have this thing going on and I understand if it turns you off. Granted, 'this thing' is an off-again on-again situation where neither of us share a genuine connection but…" She babbled and jabbered until her mouth went numb, her elbow up the whole time she did so. "I'll just go now—"

"Go? What? Why? Nevaeh." Sean gently pulled her elbows down.

Nevaeh's anxieties plummeted after recognizing his tenderness. "You don't hate me?"

"Hate you?" Sean stood with arms akimbo, one brow up and a frown on his lips. "Now, now," he spoke like a monk instructing on patience, standing calm and at ease. She searched for malice in his eyes, but there was none to be found. Hadn't he heard what she'd done? She wouldn't be fooled by this false security.

"Sean, don't act like you're not mad," Nevaeh turned her back to him and his kindness. "I led you on when there's something going on between me and someone else. Call me what you know you want to." She folded her hands as labels swarmed her mind. She'd learned his personality over the past few months, but even angels got angry.

Sean stepped around her, appearing in her line of sight, unchanged by her coldness. "Can I ask you something?"

Nevaeh dropped both arms after crossing them, observing the contemplation in his frown. She'd demanded his honesty, but feared it all the same. Was he truly angry? "Yeah. Go ahead."

Sean didn't hesitate. "Do you enjoy our lessons?"

That caught her by surprise. Of all the things to ask, why this? "Um, yes," she answered.

"And this guy is just someone you engage with when he visits?"

Nevaeh smelled his cologne when his body inched closer. She craved his sweet touch at the sight of his chest, but refused to be distracted. They were having a very necessary conversation. "Yeah. It's nothing serious, but I know to a lot of people that 'situation-ships' like ours aren't—"

"And he's not in Sweetgum right now? Sorry for cutting you off, I just need to ask." Sean scrunched up his eyes on the question, swiping the air with his hand.

Nevaeh shook her head. "He just left. But he was here like

yesterday. With the work he does, he has to travel. It's a whole thing."

"And he knows that what you two have is just a 'situationship' right? Again, just clarifying, though I'm sure he does." Sean half-smiled.

Nevaeh's tension dimmed, finding his coyness endearing. Her favorite Sean quality had to be his charm. *Nice boy charm.* She'd coined the terminology just for him. "You're right for asking because sometimes communication doesn't happen in those arrangements, so I don't blame you." His curiosity got her thinking. Rather than condemning her, he dug deep for more information. This either meant one of two things; either his brain was in shock and he was coping by using interrogation or he really liked her, but needed clarification before making a move.

She'd hate to wrongly believe the latter and ultimately hurt herself, so for now she chose to believe the former. Just for the safe-keeping of her sanity. "Yes, Matt knows that we're only on when he's here."

"Ah, got you." Sean lifted his chin in satisfaction, planting his gaze on the ceiling. "So essentially, you two are off right now."

"Yes..." she stretched out the vowel. Sean's response wasn't at all what she'd predicted, and being in the dark as he pondered made her worried yet optimistic. She wrestled with the hope that threatened to surface.

As she fret longer, Sean continued to contemplate, caressing his chin and examining the roof like a curious contractor. Suspense led to anxiety and anxiety brought a feeling of sickness. "And when he comes back, you'll be on?" he asked.

Nevaeh's eye twitched. This man and his stalling. He took pleasure in driving her mad. She could see it. He needn't spell it out. "He's my date to Brandi's wedding but right now we're off." There was nothing more to ask. Unless the particulars of Matt's occupation interested Sean.

"Nice, nice." Sean seemed ready to keep dancing but suddenly stopped, connecting their eyes in the mirror as a grin lit his face. "Can I be your date this Friday night?"

There! There it was. The payoff to this build-up. That sly fox! "Sean!" Nevaeh hit his arm as he erupted in laughter. She failed to resist her own urges and laughed loudly too, bending over and everything.

For a while it was all they did; laugh like they'd planned out the joke. She pulled herself together and watched him carry on. "You didn't strike me as the pranking type."

"Who said I was pranking you? I just wanted to know for sure how it worked." He brushed a hand over his shirt. "I know that you'd never lead me on if something serious was at play, but my friend Justin is really big on communication, so it's rubbed off on me."

"Oh, trust me, I know," Nevaeh's cheeks ached from smiling.

"So, what will it be? Friday?" A certain slickness came over him this time, weakening her muscles. Nevaeh enjoyed Sean's unassuming and sweet side, but this side reeled her in. He balanced her strong personality when gentle, but his swagger gelled well with her assertion.

She had half a mind to reject him in the name of payback, but the words couldn't leave her mouth. She'd wrapped around his finger the second he'd asked. "Yes."

CHAPTER THIRTEEN

Tonight had to go perfectly.

Sean sprayed on extra cologne for good luck and then regretted it, hoping he didn't overdo it. He combed his eyebrows in the mirror and rehearsed what he'd say. Dating after years of staying single frightened him to the point that all week, potential dating mishaps haunted his dreams.

Sean unwrapped his wave cap and told himself to simmer down. He'd gotten his hair cut at the barbershop in preparation for tonight and was pleased with the result. At least his appearance was sound, but what about his game? This was Nevaeh. They'd talked like old friends for months during their lessons, yet panic brimmed within him. The added pressure of outdoing her distant 'boyfriend' definitely contributed. He just wanted her to see what a possible relationship with him could entail. If this went south, she might never talk to Sean again.

"Ugh," he held his own face, listening to cartoons from the living room. His mom had already come in to watch Tia and the two were having a grand time on the couch. Meanwhile, his messy room mirrored his state. Discarded outfits covered the bed and shoes littered the carpet. He'd settled on one fragrance for the night, but dozens of others lay uncovered on the dresser beside his body-length mirror. Trial and error tended to breed chaos.

Sean would clean, but he'd promised to pick up Nevaeh at eight. "Got forty-five minutes until then." After putting on the finishing touch, Sean walked to the door. He hid his disappointment well, but the revelation of Matt did upset him. If not for Nevaeh's attitude while addressing their situation, his mood may not have improved. Whoever this Matt person was, he wasn't the real deal and Nevaeh knew that. Sean bet his and Nevaeh's banter during lessons electrified her more than meeting this Matt character infrequently. Competing with others never drew him in, but ever since learning of Matt, he'd gone full competitive mode with a guy he didn't even know.

"Did a twister pass through here?" His mom showed up in the doorway and coughed, pinching her nose. "How many perfumes did you spray in this room?"

Sean snatched his keys from the dresser and pocketed them. He wore black dress pants, and a white shirt with a black blazer for the evening. "It's cologne, Mom, and you could say that some sort of twister did spin around this room. The twister of indecisiveness." He put his phone in a separate pocket. "I'll clean up when I get back, but for now, I don't want to be late," he kissed her forehead. "Tia!" The child's face popped up from the couch as she kneeled in her seat. "I'm heading off, okay?"

Tia latched onto the top of the backrest and rocked back and forth. "Okay!" She climbed over and jumped to the ground, worrying Sean and his mom. "Sorry, sorry. I won't do it again." She walked on bare feet to Sean, then threw her arms around his waist, stopping him on his path to the front door. "Have a good date, Uncle Sean. Tell your lady friend that I come before her."

"Aww," said his mom by the coat rack. She buttoned her cardigan as Sean kissed Tia's face. "You'll always be Uncle's main girl."

Sean patted Tia's fuzzy head of cornrows and reminded himself to redo them soon. *That's right.* He hadn't shared with her the name of his date, but if things went well, he'd fill her in. Tonight was a trial to find out how he worked with Nevaeh outside of classes. He'd hate to excite Tia for nothing in the event it ended poorly. Sean knew how much she liked her. "Later, T and Mom. I'll see y'all around eleven." He clutched the knob and twisted it. "But by then, T will be in bed, right?" He dragged the door outward, making his way out while addressing Tia lightly.

"I won't promise a single thing," Tia smirked.

The his mother touched Tia's head and mouthed to Sean that she'd be in bed by nine.

Sean said thanks and left, accepting the well wishes they announced while jogging down the lawn. He clicked a button on his key after entering the garage and prayed that all would go well.

SOUTHERN COVE GRILL & Bistro boasted an exquisite menu of high-end seafood meals. Sweetgum unfortunately contained no branch of this marvelous restaurant chain so Sean drove Nevaeh out of town to experience it. They called Thorngale Sweetgum's distant relative. Its small, homey ambience resembled Sweetgum's aesthetic, but the presence of mainstream corporations gave it more of an urban vibe. The buildings were taller and its population quite large, but just like Sweetgum; it had friendly people ready to greet visitors with a smile.

"This is amazing." Nevaeh hadn't stopped snapping photos the second they strolled into the restaurant. She wore a white romper covered in blue florals, which Sean found breathtaking. He'd complimented her the moment he opened the car door for her to sit in the passenger seat, bringing with her an aromatic cloud. Just when he thought they'd acquainted themselves, Nevaeh went ahead and reinvented certain qualities. This time with a new perfume that differed greatly from her usual fruity fragrance. When the refreshing scent hit his nostrils, it changed his perception of her.

She wasn't just cute Nevaeh from dance class but a woman he wanted to impress. Classy, elegant and gorgeous.

Sean listened as the water lapped against the outside dock. The restaurant had a boat theme going on and was located near a body of water. They'd seen fishermen on the lake while entering the patio where patrons dined beneath the starry sky. Inside, a waiter cheerfully welcomed them and acted as a guide to their table. Due to its exclusivity, only two other couples were guests at Southern Cove Grill & Bistro tonight. White ceiling bulbs illuminated the sea-themed eating room. The pale blue walls of the sea-themed dining room had seahorse silhouettes printed in a horizontal line, while its blue carpets complemented the decor. Two violinists played a symphony by the counter.

"I know," Sean put away his phone after taking two pictures. "To be honest, I feel a little under dressed here. It's way fancier than I imagined." He took some garlic bread from the basket on their table.

Nevaeh agreed and grabbed one of her own. "You look good, though. Like, *really* good. I thought your dancing pants suited you, but this nice little blazer situation is top tier. So fresh. Ooo, and those waves," she snapped her fingers before dancing in her chair. *That was such a Neveah move*, Sean thought. "You look amazing, Sean. Like you're trying to show me up or something." She flipped a few braids to her back self-consciously.

A tingling warmth bathed Sean's face. She liked his outfit! "Thank you, Nevaeh, but it'd take looking *way* sharper than this to show *you* up. Even on an ordinary day." He'd leave it at that.

Nevaeh flicked her wrist to wave off the praise, smiling coyly. "Okay, so what are you getting? I'm more of a meat person, so all of this fish stuff is new to me," she bit into her bread.

Sean stammered at the menu. "They've got all types of fish. This is crazy."

"That soup looks good," Nevaeh finished her first slice and used a serviette to wipe her fingers. "It'd be weird if we ordered the same thing, huh?"

"Yes, for sure," Sean picked something out after finishing his appetizer. They contemplated their options. "You look like you'd enjoy their evening special. It says their forte is red snapper with a delicious curry sauce. Or, what do you think about caviar Nevaeh? Is that fancy enough for the queen herself?"

Nevaeh's mouth popped open. "Hold on. Why do you see me as this highly sophisticated sort of person?" she held up her menu to ask, her body shaking with chuckles.

Sean spread his arms while leaning backward. "You give off a queenly aura and queens are sophisticated. It's a compliment." He winked, no longer nervous and ready to wow her. They weren't at dance class, but their chemistry remained undeniable, reminding him how easy engaging with her truly was.

She batted her lashes. "Don't make me blush, Dancing Man." She put down her menu, then traced a finger along the options. "If anyone's got fancy vibes, it's you and your expertise in ballroom dancing. People don't just know that, boo."

Boo. He shot straight to heaven, kissed a cherub, and returned. Although she seemed to frequently use terms of endearment, she had never used them with him until now. He wished for more nicknames to follow. *Don't get desperate on her.* He kept it cool and went with the flow. "True. So, I guess we're royalty together, then?"

Sliding her forefinger along the laminated menu, Nevaeh gave him a sultry smile. The brief flirtation left Sean flustered.

They finally decided what to have with Nevaeh indeed choosing caviar. Some crème fraiche and lemon wedges came with the course. They thanked their waiter and dug right in.

"What do you do when you're not dancing with me in my studio?" Sean began with the usual small talk of 'getting to know you'. Despite knowing each other for months, they never delved deeper into their understanding of one another except for the time he shared his story with her. However, he was more than just his past tragedy and it seemed like she had a lot to share with him, too.

Nevaeh dabbed her lower chin. "I work at the Sweetgum Events

Committee for now but in the future, I want to have my own party planning service. Nevaeh's Heavenly Bashes!"

"I like the name. It fits since Nevaeh is heaven backwards. Although it might be catchier if the first letter of every word in the title was the same," he mixed his snapper with the rice on his plate. The flavors were to die for when they blended in his mouth. This visit would not be his last.

"You know Sean, I *did* try coming up with something like that but what word that begins with 'n' could possibly fit with parties?" She raised her glass. "It's tough out here, you know, coming up with cool names. How did you name your studio?"

He didn't want to discourage her. "I just… fused a popular saying with the word dance. Lights, Camera, Dance! Didn't take long to come up with. What? Have you been crossing names off a list since you thought of the business?" He licked his lips. The food tasted so good it was hard to eat civilly. Nevaeh somehow pulled off a perfect posture while pacing herself. He envied her self-restraint. *Maybe the caviar isn't that good.*

"Nah. I had one using my last name, but I like my first name better. Carr's Crazy Celebrations," she made quote gestures with her hands to articulate every potential name. "But 'celebrations' doesn't have that hard 'c' sound," she let out an 'mmm' on her next bite of food.

"Okay that one's pretty good but I'll admit that the first one is stuck with me. I like associating you with heaven." He came here to ensure she enjoyed herself and would stop at nothing to meet that objective. No matter the requirements, Sean would deliver.

Nevaeh's bright brown eyes widened as she whined at him to stop, this time flinging her napkin to his face. "Oh, sorry! Too much?"

"No, no, it's fine." Sean handed it back, laughing at how playful she became. He liked that side of her whenever it popped out. "So, you'll soon have a party planning business. That's cool. I'm rooting for you."

"That's the dream, but sometimes life ties our hands and ankles, so it's hard to chase them," she sighed wistfully and played with her food. For a second, those violins were all he heard. Not wanting the mood to die down, Sean moved to another topic of conversation.

"You know about—"

"How'd you—oh, sorry," she smiled sheepishly and insisted he go on.

Though his curiosity said to let her speak first, he did as she desired. "You know all about me and T. What's your family like?"

"I have a sister named India. I don't know if you've seen her around, but we grew up with our mom. My dad wasn't around. In spite of that, my childhood was... pretty good apart from when Mom got extra busy and wasn't around, but she tried her best." Nevaeh scooped a spoonful of caviar into her utensil. "What about you? I know about Tia, your um..." she hesitated to finish.

Sean shook his head. "It's okay. While I miss my sister, it's not hard to talk about her. Especially our childhood. I think we owe it to those we've lost to keep their memory alive."

Nevaeh seemed moved by this sentiment. "Right. Can I ask what she was like?"

"Of course," Sean said between bites. "As children, she was bossy, but that's older sisters for you, even if it's only by fifteen minutes."

"Ugh," Nevaeh waved a finger in his direction, shutting her eyes for emphasis, then opening them until they bulged. "Don't even get me started. Like yes, you're older, but don't boss me around. We're both children in this house."

"You know what I mean?" Sean loved that reaction. "You look like you've got some stories about India."

"Oh, we're cool now, but we used to *beef* as children," she clapped on the word 'beef.' "Sean she just—"

He was all ears, ready to take her side.

THEY SANG along to oldie goldies during their drive home. When they weren't singing, they chatted about themselves and the restaurant. Nevaeh rated it a ten out of ten, and Sean had to agree. They made a promise to visit it on a future date, which made Sean happy. The possibility of a second date excited him and meant he'd done something right. But the night wasn't over. He'd planned a scenic stroll near the lake in Sweetgum. Justin convinced him it'd set the mood for romance. With that in mind, Sean added it to their schedule as the cherry on top.

"Look at how it sparkles in the moonlight. Ah!" Nevaeh snapped photos as they walked near the lake. In the distance were hills where hikers often trailed. They seemed tiny on this street as the moon gave them light. There wasn't a cloud in the sky at this hour. He'd chosen the ideal night for this.

Sean allowed her to buzz like a kid. He considered videoing but preferred watching through his own eyes. Plus, whipping out a phone when she least expected felt wrong. "It's beautiful, isn't it?" He loved the soft grass on their feet.

"I know. Why else would I be freaking out so much?" Nevaeh happily placed her phone in her handbag, which hung off her arm. "Sometimes I wonder what it'd be like to dive in without warning. Do fish live down there?" she pointed at the sparkling waters.

"I'm guessing, yes." He scratched his head. "We might need to ask a park ranger or someone who's an expert on Sweetgum's natural resources." He walked closer to the water, tempted by its radiance. "I didn't know tonight was a full moon."

"Me neither. But it looks so amazing," she grabbed his arm. "I once saw a video where someone said how crazy it is that the moon looks really beautiful to us, but whenever we try to take a picture, our cameras *never* do it justice. Have you noticed that?" she rattled. The glowing orb above enthralled them both.

"You're right. I think the same can go for certain people." He liked her soft palms on his skin. This whole night seemed right with the universe. Was this what he'd been missing while single, or was she just extraordinary?

"Oh definitely," she trembled when a sudden breeze blew from the hills. "Guess it just goes to show that photos aren't always reliable." She tightened her grip on his arm. "Your arms feel so firm."

He flexed his biceps. "I don't always work out, but when I do, I go crazy," He winked, to which she fanned her neck playfully. They'd been at it all night, the two of them. Back-and-forth banter was their way of interacting. He rewarded himself points when he'd render her speechless or too flustered to reply. It was the cutest thing for someone so outspoken to have nothing to say.

"Oh, do you? One day you need to let me in on your secret so I can beef up too. What do you say? Help me get buff?" She couldn't finish without giggling.

Sean smiled at her silliness. "Why do you want to beef up?"

Nevaeh tiptoed to whisper in his ear. "Just to get closer to you."

Sean sucked in a breath at her closeness. "Right, of course. So, we'd be meeting for dance classes on Tuesdays and workout sessions on Wednesdays? Is that doable?" He slowed down at the bank of the lake, which stretched out much more than it seemed at first glance.

"I'd have to make time on my schedule, but yeah." She tapped his chest lightly. "I wouldn't want to be a bother. Being your dance student must have taken at least ten years off your life. Let's not take more, right?" She let go to slide her bag over her shoulder.

Sean already missed her touch, taking the adjusted bag as a sign to wrap up. It must have been late. "I actually think you *added* years, but don't quote me on that." He smiled at how the moonlight ricocheted off her enchanting brown eyes.

Nevaeh bit her bottom lip while swaying slowly toward him. "Sean."

In that moment, nothing else made sense. Not the moon or the lake or the grass on their shoes. The idea of her and what they could be consumed him, leaving him a man at her mercy. It frightened him how strong his craving for more became. More witty exchanges and compliments, more food, more walks, more of her touch. Was this his starvation of romance at play or did Nevaeh just do things to him? "Yeah?"

"This is so incredible. Thanks for taking me to the lake. It— oh my goodness, ducks! They stay awake this long? Sean!" Nevaeh snatched his wrist and gestured to a handful of ducks swimming to the bank. "Do you see this?"

"I do, I do. Wish I had some bread. They're probably hungry." He heard their small 'quacks' and laughed. "Tia would love this."

"Oh, if we come back another time, we should bring her along. Ugh, it'd be so cute to watch her feed ducks— okay, they're coming too close," She hid behind him and shooed them off. "Birds creep me out."

Sean felt her nails scrape at his back as she gripped the back of his shirt. They tickled, and he laughed at the sensation and her sudden flip in attitude. This girl was the greatest, and no one could convince him otherwise.

In the end, he drove Nevaeh home to her apartment complex. At her door, an uncomfortable silence fell. Their wonderful night had come to a close.

Sean fought the heartbreak that threatened him. "Tonight was fun." He put his hands in his pockets. "It's nearly midnight, and I bet my mom's fallen asleep on my couch."

Nevaeh laughed tiredly at the light joke. "I had a lot of fun, too, Sean." She averted her eyes from his and instead looked at the door. "I guess I'll see you next Tuesday?"

"Yeah," Sean already began the countdown. "Next Tuesday."

The emptiness of the hallway only amplified the sadness he felt at the thought of saying goodbye. Sean would hate for tonight to end flat, so he allowed his instincts to lead him.

Heart racing, he closed the gap between them, catching her by surprise. He leaned in, planting a quick kiss on her lips. The electricity it sparked nearly knocked him off his feet.

A warmth spread through him as their lips met. Her lips were soft, their kiss a quiet promise. He pulled back to find her eyes closed, a small, satisfied smile on her face like she was savoring the memory of their kiss.

He stepped back, watching her under the dull hallway light. Her cheeks were flushed, her eyes still closed, like she was soaking up the last few seconds of the moment.

When she finally opened her eyes, he noticed something different. There was a softness, a glow in her gaze he hadn't seen before. Their first kiss was innocent but powerful, a simple act that held a world of unspoken promises. It felt like the beginning of something real, something special.

Sean waved as he continued moving backward. "Good night, Nevaeh. Have a good one." He turned around without another word.

CHAPTER FOURTEEN

"Nevaeh, ice doves are always a safe bet," Brandi remarked, sharing a Saturday brunch with her friend. They had rendezvoused at Rochelle's Old Fashioned Diner to reconnect and strategize. The remnants of bagels and raspberries that once occupied their plate were now nothing but a memory. The pair had devoured them absent-mindedly while their minds navigated through wedding plans. The big day was quickly approaching, and the list of unfinished tasks seemed never-ending.

Heaving a sigh, Brandi turned a page in her scrapbook, her brows creased in thought. They sat in their favorite booth. There were only four other people there, so it felt like they had the place to themselves. The stillness of the morning, punctuated by sporadic beams of sun flitting through the entrance, felt like the perfect invitation to be outdoors. But duty called—they had a wedding to plan. "Ice doves might overdo it, though," Brandi mused. "What about an ice… fish?"

The absurdity of an ice fish sculpture at a reception made Nevaeh grimace. "No, let's stick to the doves, Brandi. You're getting all twisted up over little things. You've always had a soft spot for doves, remember?"

"I guess you're right," Brandi relented, glancing at her scrapbook. She paused thoughtfully and turned the page. "Oh, by the way, your date with Sean was last night, wasn't it? Her expression lightened up when she mentioned Nevaeh's date.

Memories from the lavish caviar dinner to the electrifying good-night kiss resurfaced, inducing a flurry of butterflies in Nevaeh's stomach. "Yes, I went out with Sean," she confirmed, her gaze falling on a photo of stunning bridesmaid dresses.

"And?" Brandi probed, bouncing in her seat, barely concealing her excitement. "You were so nervous before the date, but now you're holding back on the details. Did things not go as planned?" The smile on Brandi's face faltered.

"No, no, it was amazing! Sean...he's something else," Nevaeh insisted, her body tingling at the thought of him. "I'm just trying to collect my thoughts. That kiss… it still gives me butterflies."

Brandi gasped, her features frozen in a mix of surprise and elation. "He kissed you!" she exclaimed, clutching Nevaeh's hands.

"Yes!" Nevaeh met Brandi's enthusiasm with a gentle squeeze of their entwined hands. "Yes, he kissed me. It was brief but magical. But now what? He did mention us seeing each other again." The feel of his kiss lingered on her lips, its sweet memory accompanying her to the diner that morning.

"Then see him again, Nevaeh. It's clear there's a spark between you two." Brandi leaned over her scrapbook, her voice taking a serious tone. "You've deserved a real, honest relationship for a while now. It's time to let Matt go. He has shown time and again that he doesn't value you the way he should."

Nevaeh's friends, Joanne and Courtney, echoed the same sentiment in their group chats. She was so used to brushing aside Matt's emotional neglect, but her expectations had shifted after experiencing Sean's affectionate attention. Was it fair to demand more from Matt now? Maybe this was a sign that she needed to seek a more meaningful relationship. She should stop settling for less and demand more from her partner.

"You're right, Brandi." A group of teenagers entering the diner interrupted her train of thought, their chatter filling the air. A delicious aroma wafted from the kitchen, the scent of fresh cherry pie luring her back to reality. "I think I want to see where things go with Sean."

"That's the spirit, Nevaeh," Brandi replied, giving her a thumbs up. "Just make sure your fling with Matt finally meets its deserved end," she teased, nudging Nevaeh playfully. Her warm smile comforted Nevaeh, reassuring her that she was on the right path.

"Now, back to this wedding business. It's crunch time!" Nevaeh's attention returned to the scrapbook as Brandi straightened up, ready to dive back into wedding preparations.

SATURDAYS WERE Nevaeh's designated grocery shopping days. Cruising down the familiar aisles of the grocery store, she often crossed paths with coworkers and acquaintances doing their weekend restocking. While the early morning rush turned the store into a battleground of crowded carts, Nevaeh was smart enough to avoid it by shopping in the afternoon. Her phone flashed 2:30, and the dwindling number of customers around her confirmed the hour. The employee restocking the snacks aisle gave a salute and she nodded back while pushing her cart.

Between helping Brandi with wedding details, navigating her growing feelings for Sean, and combating her own dance-related insecurities, Nevaeh felt emotionally drained. After heaving a heavy milk carton into her cart, she surveyed the other items already gathered—oil, flour, eggs, fruits—not many more things remained on her list. An overwhelming desire washed over her to finish up, head home, and just bury herself in her bed. The dread that seized her whenever she pictured herself dancing horribly and stealing the limelight at Brandi's wedding was tiring. Perhaps sleep could wait.

She needed to practice dancing more than she needed to rest. *Yeah, sleep can wait until night,* she reasoned.

As she tossed a few frozen pizzas into her cart, a slight patter of footsteps echoed from the next aisle.

"Uncle Sean, look! It's Nevaeh!" She was shocked to see Sean and little Tia walking towards her. Tia's bright eyes sparkled with excitement upon seeing Nevaeh, while Sean flashed her a warm smile from behind his cart.

Nevaeh froze for a moment. Seeing Sean so unexpectedly, so soon after their date, felt strange. Thoughts of their tender kiss the previous night flitted through her mind, leaving her momentarily speechless. How was she supposed to act around him now?

"Nevaeh, you look beautiful even on Saturdays!" Tia's tiny frame crashed into Nevaeh's legs as she enveloped her in a tight hug.

"T! Manners!" Sean chastised gently, pulling Tia away. He apologized to Nevaeh with an embarrassed smile. "She blurts out the most random things. Although," he ruffled Tia's head of curls affectionately, "she's not wrong."

Nevaeh smiled at the innocent compliment. "Thanks, Tia. I always say it's important to look good. You never know who you might bump into," she replied playfully, sending Sean a cheeky look.

Sean's charming grin widened. "That's a fair point. So, Nevaeh, do you always shop in the afternoon to beat the morning rush?"

"That's smart! Uncle Sean and I do the same thing," Tia chirped, twirling happily before suddenly making a spontaneous proposition. "You should come to our house for dinner, Nevaeh! We're having Italian tonight!" She enthusiastically held up a packet of spaghetti and ground beef from Sean's cart.

Sean seemed caught off guard. "Dinner? Tia, don't be silly. I'm sure Nevaeh already has plans for tonight." He gave Nevaeh a pointed look.

Nevaeh quickly picked up on the hint and played along, "Yeah, a last-minute dinner might be a bit... unexpected, don't you think,

Tia?" Sean had been clear on their date that Tia wasn't aware of their romantic involvement, which Nevaeh completely understood.

Tia, however, was undeterred. "I know, but it's perfect! I mean, you guys went out last night, right? What's the big deal about a second date?" Tia said, spreading her arms wide in triumph, causing Sean and Nevaeh to stare open-mouthed.

In utter disbelief, Nevaeh turned to Sean, who was struggling to keep his composure. "Tia," he muttered, glancing at Nevaeh apologetically, "That's not... you can't just... there are boundaries." He tried to chastise her, but Tia looked downcast.

"But Uncle Sean, I think it would be nice if—" Tia started to argue but was interrupted by Nevaeh.

"Well, you know what?" Nevaeh said, pointing a finger at Tia. "I think I *will* come over for dinner." The look of complete joy on Tia's face warmed her heart.

Tia turned to Sean with pleading eyes. "Uncle Sean, please? I know I messed up, but Nevaeh wants to come. Can she?" She tugged at Sean's t-shirt, her eyes wide with hope.

Sean broke into a grin as he studied Nevaeh. "You want to? Well, sure, why not? You like pasta, right?" He quickly caught Tia's arm when she began skipping around in excitement.

"Who doesn't?" Nevaeh replied. As Sean and Tia bid their good-byes and walked away, the reality of what she'd just agreed to finally sank in. Was this moving too fast?

⁂

NEVAEH HAD ALWAYS BEEN quick to adapt; it was her strong suit, her lifeline in unfamiliar territory. Tonight, at dinner, that trait would be more of a necessity than an asset. A home-cooked meal after a first date was a move that could throw anyone off their rhythm, and Nevaeh was no exception. As she stood on Sean's doorstep, she sent up a silent prayer, hoping she could keep her anxiety under wraps, preserving the confident façade she worked so hard to maintain.

Nevaeh had been gripped by anxiety about this dinner, a feeling that only began to dissolve once Sean opened the door to his home, his warm welcome immediately putting her at ease. The large rooms of his one-story house contrasted starkly with her smaller apartment across town, yet they seemed perfectly fitting for a pair like Sean and Tia.

As she entered, she was immediately drawn to the three-seated sofa, an inviting centerpiece in the living room, and the sleek TV stand nearby. Family photographs were neatly arranged on the stand, but Nevaeh's preoccupied mind didn't allow her the opportunity to pause and examine them closely.

In the dining room, an already set table awaited her. Tia, matching Sean's enthusiastic greeting, added a touch of personal care by presenting her with a specially folded napkin. They gathered around the small wooden table, a sense of warm camaraderie enveloping the room.

Ever the gracious hostess, Tia promised to give Nevaeh a tour of her room once the meal finished. But, already, from what she had seen, Nevaeh found herself increasingly charmed by the place.

"And you know what she said after that?" Tia's plate was clean; not a single morsel of food remained. The conversation flowed easily, and eating with Sean and Tia gave her the same feeling as catching up with her girlfriends.

Sean faced Nevaeh, concealing laughter that was fighting to break free. He sometimes finished Tia's sentences when she recounted past school drama, but the child whined when he did. Tia was eager to tell Nevaeh everything she had shared with Sean during the school year. Nevaeh liked that she tried to include her.

"Uncle Sean, don't tell her," Tia wagged her fork at her uncle.

When Sean put a finger on his lips, Nevaeh wrapped the remnants of her spaghetti around her fork. She and Sean sat in front of Tia, who took the single chair on the other side. "What did she say, T? I'm all ears." This elementary school tea had her hooked.

Back in her day she'd met some mean children, too, so Tia's tales hardly surprised her.

Tia's little eyes squinted, and her face scrunched in fury. She meant business with that expression, but it looked so adorable Nevaeh barely took her seriously. "She said don't touch my sparkly pencils again or I'll call my cousin to put you in your place!"

Nevaeh snapped her fingers consecutively around her face. "As she should. I'm glad she stood up for herself and that you gave the advice to do that. Some people need the extra push." Nevaeh stood up to extend her hand across the table.

Tia high-fived her, then went in for their secret handshake. "I know. I'm a good friend."

Nevaeh sat and turned to the softly laughing Sean. "What's so funny? That situation was life or death, Sean. These children need to learn to protect their belongings." She nudged his rib in a teasing manner.

"Uncle Sean likes laughing at my stories, but you don't. So, right now I like you better, Nevaeh." Tia bared missing teeth in a precious little smile.

Sean gasped audibly as Nevaeh said, "I'm always here for you, baby. Women's stories matter. Even when the women who tell them are still growing into themselves, that's when they matter the most."

Sean rolled his eyes at Nevaeh and extended one finger to the sassy little girl. "Tia, this is the first time I've ever laughed at your stories, and it's because you told me to keep quiet. So technically, I'm not laughing." He straightened his shirt. "Nevaeh, don't see me as the villain in this situation. I love this girl and give her all the attention she needs. And yes, I do take her stories seriously." He made a face at Tia, who crossed her eyes his way. They began a silly face contest which Nevaeh joined in on, entertaining the little girl who had them both wrapped around her fingers.

Nevaeh smiled openly when they ended the competition. Tia rose to show Nevaeh her room, but a sudden knock sounded at the front door. "Expecting anyone?" Nevaeh asked.

Sean looked blank, but Tia's eyes twinkled with mischief. "Are... *you* expecting someone, T?" he asked with a frown.

The child practically catapulted from her chair and ran for the door. "Oh, no one important."

Nevaeh and Sean watched as she raced to the door. Sean looked kind of worried, but Tia certainly wasn't. Nevaeh got the feeling a prank was in the works. As long as it left her clothes clean, she'd be a good sport. Not that a seven-year-old could possibly orchestrate anything that diabolical. "Who do you think it is?" she asked Sean.

Sean stood with a shrug just as Tia pulled the door open. "I don't know. Let me—Mom and Dad?" His eyebrows shot to the top of his forehead, a genuine display of stun. "What are—"

"Sean," they said at the same time.

Nevaeh straightened her clothes automatically and wiped her mouth with her napkin. Without thinking, she got up to stroke her braids and plaster on a smile. She was meeting his parents *and* seeing his house in the same night after only one date? This had to be a record. "Mr. and Mrs. Martin." Was her smile intact? Did she seem amicable enough?

The elderly couple strode into the room hand in hand. Tia fidgeted next to them, bouncing from one foot to the other. "I'll get my jacket!" she called, running to her bedroom with no explanation as to why she would do such a thing.

"You guys are here and Tia just left for her coat, so..." Sean stuttered and stammered.

"Didn't Tia tell you she'd be coming with us for ice cream after dinner this evening?" his mom said, then turned to Nevaeh. "You're his new student? *Wow,* quite the looker. Tia was right!" She hooked her arm in her husband's. "Sean you—"

Sean babbled rapid nonsense to get his mom to be quiet. It amused Nevaeh to no end. "Yup. I'm the new girl. Wait, so Tia arranged to go out for ice cream after dinner? Did she tell you that?" she asked, turning to Sean.

Judging by Sean's agape mouth and blinking eyes, Nevaeh

guessed he'd been left out of these plans. "No. I never said she could—"

"I'm back and all set!" Tia pranced up to her grandparents, wearing a purple hoodie. She shrugged the hood onto her head, then held her grandfather's hand. "Now let's go, guys. Remember, after ice cream, we have to watch movies." Her eyes flickered with playfulness. "Before I sleep over, of course," she laughed.

Nevaeh switched her gaze from Sean to Tia too many times to count. "So… she's leaving?"

"You didn't tell your uncle?" Sean's father looked just about as lost as Sean—if that were possible. "Wait a second. Is something else going on that we're unaware of?" his wrinkly eyes narrowed. "Wait…" he lowered his body, then whispered in Tia's ear.

The child mouthed 'bingo' then waved. "Anyway. You two have fun. Oh, Nevaeh, these are my grandparents. Shake hands before we leave. We don't have all night. Tick tock and chop, chop." Tia clapped her little hands while Nevaeh introduced herself more formally. "All right, now we go! Bye Uncle Sean and Nevaeh!" She laughed deviously while trailing the old couple to the door. They hurriedly said goodbye and took their leave.

And now, the only occupants of the house were Nevaeh and her dance instructor. They exchanged looks for a second, but she broke eye contact soon after, trying not to collapse at the drastic turn of events. "We should…"

"I'll clean up and then maybe we can… watch a movie?" Sean suggested while lifting his plate.

The tension broke, allowing her to breathe clearer. "Sounds good. Let me help."

CHAPTER FIFTEEN

The movie was an old-school gem from the nineties, a horror flick Sean cherished from his childhood. It was amusing that Nevaeh had picked it when he'd offered up their choices. It wasn't every day you met a woman as stunning, charismatic, and easygoing as Nevaeh, who shared your love for all things chilling and thrilling.

They had dimmed the lights; apart from the soft glow of the living room's flat screen, the rest of his home basked in darkness, reminiscent of a movie theater. On Nevaeh's playful suggestion, they'd made popcorn, and now a bowl of it sat invitingly on the coffee table.

They settled comfortably on the couch, shoes tossed aside for the utmost relaxation. Without any prompting, Nevaeh nestled herself against Sean, and he felt like everything in his world was settling into place.

Five times already, Nevaeh had buried her face in his arm, hiding from the movie's ghastly creatures, only to laugh at her own scare-induced squeals. That laugh was Sean's kryptonite; he thanked his lucky stars he was seated, or he'd be a goner.

"You'd never guess I've watched this a thousand times, huh?"

Nevaeh nabbed the popcorn bowl, her fingers deftly grabbing a handful, then munching on the kernels one at a time.

"A thousand?" Sean leaned back into the comfortable embrace of his plush gray couch, the cushions molding to his form at his slightest movement. "You've got one up on me. I watched it often growing up, but it wasn't always my go-to for horror," he admitted, a surge of delight racing through him as she cuddled further into his chest. "That part wasn't so bad," he protested at the sight of a monstrous octopus making a meal of someone's legs on the screen. "Okay, yeah, scratch that."

Forcing herself to peek through her fingers at the grotesque scene, Nevaeh abandoned the attempt immediately and buried her face back into his chest. "Wait, what was your top pick then?" she asked, lifting her face.

Her eyes, captivating brown jewels, mesmerized him. The flickering TV light didn't do them justice. She was close, but not close enough. Why this sudden yearning? It buzzed through him, heating him from the inside. "The sequel to this one," he said, draping his arm around her shoulders. Would she accept his overture?

Her response was warm and encouraging as she leaned further into his embrace. To his delight, she grabbed his hand. As she intertwined their fingers, he felt her weight shift as she swung her legs over his lap. Their comfort with each other felt innate, like a rhythm established over countless past lifetimes. "Yes. That sequel is insane," she said, her voice low.

"You're telling me. I love how the octopus inexplicably has offspring that decide to devour the entire planet instead of just the town." Sean idly twisted a strand of her braid around his finger. "They completely lean into the ludicrous horror movie trope, and it's fantastic."

Laughing, Nevaeh agreed, "I know, right? Why are bad movies sometimes so much better than good ones?" She rested her head on his shoulder, looking up at him.

Resisting the sudden urge to lean in for a kiss, Sean replied, "I enjoy good movies too, the ones that sweep the awards with their riveting plots and performances." On screen, the military was taking on the octopus monster, its long, slimy tentacles tossing their tanks aside. It was now up to the protagonists to use their near-death experiences with the creature to put an end to its reign. Predictable plotlines, but he never got tired of them.

"I mean, don't get me wrong, I love getting teary at a well-crafted scene. There's this indie movie—maybe you haven't heard of it—where this kid was playing with his little sister and she got hurt. He spends his whole life consumed with guilt even though it wasn't his fault..."

As she described the plot, Sean felt a jolt of recognition. "Wait, in the climax, does his mom finally lose it and give him a reality check?" he asked, interrupting her.

Nevaeh's reaction was electric. "Yes! You've watched it too!" Her joy was infectious, her surprise palpable. Even the playful slap she delivered to his chest in her excitement was endearing. "I'm sorry, boo," she apologized, leaning in to kiss it better, her soft lips making Sean's heart flutter. "Why'd you watch that, Sean? Wait, I see what you're doing," Nevaeh continued, poking his nose lightly. "You've been getting an inside scoop on me from Courtney, huh? Trying to impress me tonight. Nice move, Dancing Man. I'm impressed."

Sean brought a finger to her lips, leaning closer. "Nevaeh?" Their lips were barely a breath apart. "Remember, this entire dinner just sort of happened. I wouldn't have had time to plot with your friend. Plus, that's not my style," he said as she shivered. He felt it, too. It was like an electric current sparking in the living room.

Nevaeh seemed taken aback, stumbling over her words. In the soft glow of the TV, he admired the light playing on her cheeks. Would she respond, or had he rendered her speechless?

In a sudden move, she closed her eyes and pulled him closer, her hands cupping his face as she kissed him passionately. Sean matched her rhythm, their movements in perfect sync. Sean's heart raced as her fingers ran through his hair, and he pulled her onto his lap, facing him as they remained locked in their embrace. The next thing he knew, they were navigating their way to his bedroom, his arms cradling her like the treasure she was. Tonight, he would be her willing devotee.

CRACK! Pop! Crackle!

The next morning, Sean diced onions beside the stove, wearing only his pajama pants. The sound of chirping sparrows filled the air as he gazed out the over-sink window. The pure blue horizon seemed to stretch on forever, giving the sun ample space to shine brilliantly. Sean savored the moment, enjoying the tranquility of the Sunday morning.

"It's going to burn if you don't put the rest of the ingredients in," Nevaeh called over her shoulder. His T-shirt stretched past her toned thighs like a dress, and he had to admit that she rocked that old shirt better than he ever could. He had half a mind to tell her to keep it. But, he also had a sudden desire to forget about breakfast completely, and… No, he had to snap out of it and not be distracted. He was sure Nevaeh was quite hungry after their prolonged shower that morning.

Sean apologized for his slowness and moved to her side to scrape all the onions into the pan. "Are you sure this way's the best one? I always season before pouring my eggs in."

He tucked a loose strand of her braid behind her ear; she'd tied them up for breakfast. However she opted to wear it made no difference to him. Although … he did like the sight of her neck. Her baby hairs curled at the base of her scalp over clear skin. He pinched at the golden necklace he saw peeping from under her collar. *My collar.*

Nevaeh made good use of the wooden spoon she'd selected. She stir-fried the mixture with ease as a heavenly aroma rose from the pan. "Of course. What? Don't you watch cooking shows?" She turned up the heat under the eggs. "Learned this method from the best of the best. You've been doing it all wrong, Sean."

She scrambled their breakfast to pure magnificence, then lifted her arm and dropped her spoon dramatically into the pan. "There you have it. No flaws, just delectable eggs made by yours truly," she said as she posed with one hand on her hip and the other making a peace sign.

Sean took a deep breath, restraining himself from embracing her. He chose to try her creation instead, being sure to do so dramatically. "I'll be the judge of that."

Shing! Their bread popped up from the toaster, startling Nevaeh, who hurried to butter them. "No, wait! Wait until we sit and eat. Come on, Sean, don't be impatient."

"All right, all right," Sean dropped the spoon. "Let me help out," he went to the drawer for a butter knife of his own.

These had to be the best eggs he'd ever tasted! Sean sat back in great satisfaction as a smug Nevaeh held up her juice in salute.

"Call me when you need a real egg master, okay?"

Sean lifted his cup. "Oh, I will. Certainly. No question about it." He drank his orange juice, more satisfied from a meal than he'd been in quite some time. It wasn't just about the food, though. She just completed him in a way he didn't realize he needed.

That puzzle from before. Himself, Tia, and a missing portion. Was she it? With these thoughts in mind, he thought of his niece. He'd call his parents soon, to check on her, but for now, he contemplated the notion of Nevaeh as an addition.

During dinner last night, he'd never doubted that Tia appreciated Nevaeh's presence, but inviting her over and moving her in wasn't on the same level. And why was he thinking about this so soon?

Knock, knock, knock.

"You going to get that, or should I?" Nevaeh asked when Sean didn't move.

He got up suddenly reminded of his lack of clothes. "Shoot! Let me get a shirt on really quick," he said as he dashed to his bedroom, rolling his eyes when Nevaeh cackled. He liked how comfortable she'd become. As far as he could see, she made no attempt to suppress any aspects of her personality. *That laugh.* He smiled while grabbing himself a shirt.

As Sean pulled on a t-shirt, he heard high-pitched chattering in the living room. Had Nevaeh answered already? *In just a T-shirt?* He became hot in the face at the idea of Tia asking questions. *I think she's already doing that.* "Hang on!" Sean's feet stomped upon his carpet when he dashed out the door.

Sean was met by the sight of Tia and Nevaeh sharing a hug. "Oh, T. Did Grandma and Grandpa drop you off?" he'd heard his mother while getting ready.

Tia let go of Nevaeh to wave. "Uncle Sean. You're only wearing sleeping clothes, too! Did I miss a new game?" The clothes she had on were not the same ones she had been wearing before. His parents' house had two drawers dedicated solely to Tia's spare outfits.

Nevaeh patted Tia's head. "Oh, nothing you should worry about, little T. Just adults doing boring adult things." She winked at Sean, probably amused with herself.

"I know what I missed!" Tia ran to the kitchen and scowled. She pointed to their empty plates. "You two had breakfast without me. Uncle Sean and Nevaeh, why did you make eggs when you know they're my favorite?" she crossed her small arms with a shake of her head. "We could have had so much fun eating eggs as a family, but I guess not."

"Aww, T!" Nevaeh rushed in to comfort her, pulling the child to her body. "Next time, okay? But you did have breakfast at Grandma's, right?" she pinched Tia's chubby cheeks.

"Yup! Oh, will you stay for lunch? Maybe we can have that together."

"I mean, I was going to go home to change, but I can come back to spend the rest of Sunday here if you want me to."

"Yes! You and Uncle Sean had your fun, so now it's my turn. Yay!"

"Woohoo!"

Sean could watch them talk forever. That puzzle analogy returned, but this time as a complete picture where Nevaeh fit perfectly. She and Tia cleared the table, conversing effortlessly as they worked. *Like a real family.* He thought of Tia's words. "I'll wipe down the table for you guys," he finished the puzzle by adding himself, transforming this scene into a family at work after breakfast.

CHAPTER SIXTEEN

"Another day, another dance disaster." Nevaeh fought hard to keep up with Tia's steps, as Tia pretended to be her dance partner. The lights radiated overhead as usual, and the floors almost tripped her. Never had she encountered them unwaxed. This time, she even caught her reflection in the wood.

"*Pam, pam, pa!*" Tia assigned each move a sound to assist Nevaeh's efforts. "You almost had it this time—ow!" She jumped when Nevaeh stomped on her foot.

"Sorry!" Nevaeh let go to swoop her off her feet. She kissed Tia's cheek, then put her back down. "Baby, I am *so* sorry. See? That's why I told you not to bother. I'm a mess!" She grabbed the end of her hoodie and dragged it over her face in frustration. Brandi's wedding was almost here, and Nevaeh wasn't prepared. "You know what's going to happen?" She whined after uncovering her face.

Tia blinked at her with large brown eyes. "What?" She took Nevaeh's hand, swinging it in hers.

"I'm going to get on that dance floor at Brandi's wedding and make a fool of myself! And when I do that, I'll steal all the attention away from her, since everyone will laugh at me." She buried her face in her hands to groan melodramatically. "It's hopeless, I say. Hopeless! *Agh!*" She punched the air like it personally offended her.

"You're being more dramatic than me, and I'm seven," Tia scolded. Sean was having an impromptu meeting with one of the parents so Tia was helping her out. Nevaeh wished he'd come back soon. "Don't start whining now, Nevaeh," Tia wagged her finger. "If you really want to make your friend happy, then crying about how bad you are won't help." She placed her feet on top of Nevaeh's, then took her hands a second time. "Let's try again, but this time with my feet on yours so you don't step on me." Her solution so endeared Nevaeh that she decided to go with it.

Tia provided the music by singing a popular waltz. With Tia's feet on hers, Nevaeh felt responsible for keeping her steady, which was a very terrifying concept for the clumsiest person to ever stumble the planet Earth. Her nerves got the best of her, and she tripped on a step, sending them both crashing to the ground.

Nevaeh had promptly broken Tia's fall by positioning herself beneath the child's body. "Are you okay?"

Tia laughed hysterically, then took Nevaeh's arm. "That was fun, but let's try again without tripping. Just follow my lead." She rolled away from Nevaeh and stood abruptly. With an outstretched hand, she helped Nevaeh up and went over each step.

From here, all Nevaeh did was watch, completely mystified. This infant was showing her up. *Even an electrocuted dog could show me up with the moves I got.* That being none. But Tia had talent. She danced with as much grace as Sean and wasted no energy when taking form. The little girl did it with ease, too, stepping and twirling when the choreography called for such. If only she'd been blessed with such grace.

"Now you," Tia called, beckoning to Nevaeh. "We're not leaving until you get this. Everyone can dance. Even clumsy people like you, Nevaeh. You just have to try and believe!" She hopped aside and bounced in place, watching Nevaeh begin. "I'll sing so you don't get confused."

Nevaeh hid her self-consciousness behind a forced laugh. "Okay then. Just let me do some stretches before I try on my own."

"We stretched already. Time to dance! One-two-three, one-two-three…" Tia clapped and tapped her foot to cue Nevaeh in.

The uncoordinated woman asked for strength from above, then imitated Tia's flow the best that she could. Sean had taught Nevaeh these moves too many times to count. If she messed up, she deserved jail time. There wasn't much to it.

She began with folded lips, unsteadily matching Tia's timing while waltzing with no partner. She struggled on some steps, but Tia urged her to ignore that and dance to the best of her ability. The child gently advised Nevaeh to close her eyes, which showed how similar she was to her uncle in her compassion and patience.

Nevaeh took the suggestion and held her lids shut. She even hummed along to Tia's song, giving a hundred and ten percent to her execution. She could do it. The steps were all there. She had practiced them like crazy; now, she just had to solidify them. She had to. For Sean, for Tia, and for Brandi, too.

The heat of another body suddenly bombarded her, holding her upper waist with a tenderness she recognized. His scent, shape, and swift gliding soothed her soul and alighted her body. "Sean," Nevaeh opened her eyes and stared at the man she adored. His kind smile lit up his face and made her heart skip a beat. When did he get here? She spotted Tia grinning away. They must have planned to surprise her while her eyes had been closed.

"Hey, Nev. You weren't bad at all just now. A little jumpy, but we can fix that." He spun her around, and the room was a blur of color and movement. Then he brought the dance to a halt. "Thank you, T, for being our DJ, but I think my phone might be a better pick in terms of music." He waved it around, and the girl ran to take it. "You want to get the waltz music for us?" he smirked at Nevaeh. He'd gotten ten times more attractive since their first date.

"Yup!" Tia swiped through the songs before music blared from Sean's speakers. "Twenty-four-hour waltz music. It reminds me of the princess movie we watched on Sunday. Do you remember that, Nevaeh?" Tia beamed and sprang like a bunny. That habit of hers always got Nevaeh. Could a child be any cuter?

"Of course, I remember. That movie was bomb." Nevaeh took Sean's hands, meeting his eyes with hers as jitters suddenly swaddled her. "When the music starts, I tend to get flustered."

That fact seemed to make absolutely no difference to Sean. With an air of understanding, he pulled Nevaeh in. "I just want to dance with you."

Everything went hot. Nevaeh's sweatshirt trapped her in an inferno of heat that froze over at the smile that followed. *What is he doing to me?* she thought as she let the music take over.

The waltzes played on, and Nevaeh and Sean kept dancing. It didn't matter that Nevaeh squashed Sean's toes now and again; he simply laughed when she apologized, continuing to glide her across the room.

Tia twirled around them with pristine ballet technique, improvising incredible leaps which fit the songs. While Nevaeh liked having her present as backup, Sean eventually made her leave. His reason being she'd miss a certain online program if she didn't. Before she ran off, the dynamic girl gave Nevaeh a heartfelt hug.

After what seemed like forever, Sean decided it was time for a break. The sound of the music from his speaker filled the room. As he brushed the sweat from his face, Nevaeh couldn't help but notice the way his muscles rippled beneath his shirt. "I think you're getting the hang of it," said Sean through heavy breaths. He smiled from ear to ear. "My toes aren't as numb as they usually are at all our other classes. That means you've stepped on them less." He gave a thumbs up and patted her arm.

Nevaeh pushed Sean's chest. "Shut up. If you're making fun of me, I'm not having it, Sean." She feigned offense, and he hastily explained that he meant it as praise. Nevaeh knew that, but liked messing around. For some reason, a spirit of playfulness currently possessed her. More than anything, she yearned to bask in this moment before time ran out. They'd had such a ball last weekend; could they do that now? Just *be* in the presence of one another?

"... but I understand that I phrased that wrongly. What I wanted to say was..." Another song started, and he took her by the waist. "You've made impressive strides towards improvement and I'm proud," he said.

Nevaeh nuzzled him after putting both arms on Sean's shoulders. "Thank you. I practice a lot *and* I have a good teacher," she said as she started over, taking the lead this time. "I promise you I won't make mistakes."

"Oh— okay. Don't put too much pressure on yourself. We still have time until the wedding. About three weeks, right?" He made room as she carefully got through four moves. "Would you look at that?"

Nevaeh squealed at his pride but wished he'd shut up. "I don't want to lose focus." With her eyes fixed on the ground, she navigated smoothly without any hiccups. "Your toes are getting a break." She watched him laugh, then scrunched up her nose. "You're laughing, but I'm dead serious. This time will be different. See? So far I'm getting it." She nearly kicked him in the shin but stopped impact just in time.

He intertwined their fingers after connecting their hands for a more formal approach. Sean stroked her waist, and she grabbed hold of his shoulder. "If you make it through, I might just present you a gift," he winked smartly, guiding every motion made so Nevaeh didn't trip.

Nevaeh feared harming him while keeping up the conversation. "A gift? For me? I'll be really cheesy and say dancing with you right now is gift enough."

Sean mimicked her signature pout. The exaggerated impression made her heart soar. "That's actually really sweet, but I think you'd deserve something more special for everything you're doing right now. I mean, look at us."

They glided across the dance floor like professionals—by

Nevaeh's standards, anyway. She was amazed by how well she had executed the choreography, having never come close to doing anything like it before. She determinedly gave everything not to ruin it. *Only a few more parts to go,* she thought, paying close attention.

"I should have perfected this since lesson fifty," Nevaeh's foot bucked against his, but she saved it before ruining what they had, telling herself that didn't count. They side-walked to the front mirrors, did the same thing backwards, and finally ended with Sean giving her a twirl. The music paused just before another waltz tune began, this one jumpier than the last. It amazed Nevaeh how every one of them were waltzes but varied so drastically.

He spun her back towards him so they faced each other. With a grin radiating fulfillment, he brushed a kiss against her lips. "Well done." He let go to applaud, cheering her on for what she accomplished.

Nevaeh bent forward and saw sweat droplets falling. They wet Sean's polished wood but were a sign of hard work. "The queen is back, baby!" She stood tall and shot fists in the air. "I did that, didn't I?" She freestyled something goofy, but didn't care how it looked.

It had taken many lessons. Many *grueling* lessons of agony before it all came together. "It's because I never gave up."

"You never did. You never ever did, and I'm proud," Sean said, pulling her in for a hug. "I *really* need to get you something for your efforts. I know I keep saying it, Nevaeh, but I don't think you understand just how proud I am of you," he said as he smiled. They'd achieved this together after weeks of hard work.

Nevaeh felt tears in her eyes that threatened to fall. "Why'd you even say that? Now I'm about to cry like a baby over doing something I should have done a long time ago," she gave a soft laugh.

Sean looked at her intently, his eyes darkening, and the air between them growing heavy with unspoken words. He pulled her closer, his hands gentle but firm, and brushed her hair out of her face. Her breath caught as his fingers lingered on her skin, and he gently raised her chin, his eyes locked with hers.

She could feel his breath on her face as he leaned in, his lips barely touching hers, teasing and testing. The moment seemed to stretch forever, neither one willing to break the connection. Finally, his lips met hers, soft and tentative at first, then growing more confident.

He seemed reluctant to pull away, and she felt a deep sense of loss at the removal of his touch. "Let me turn this off to pack up," Sean referred to his blasting music, his voice rough with emotion. He hesitated again, his eyes never leaving hers, but eventually went to grab his phone. "Got a long workday tomorrow, Nevaeh?"

She went for her things, her hands trembling slightly. Nevaeh shoved her bottled water into her backpack, but her mind was on the heat of his touch, the taste of his lips. "Yes, I do," she said, her voice barely above a whisper. "And I'm guessing the same goes for you, huh?" she asked as Sean walked back over to her.

"Yup," he smiled down at her, his eyes still intense. "But you gave me energy to face the rest of the week," he said softly, touching a finger to her upper chest. His touch sent a shiver through her. "Don't worry. You might just be in for something sweet next time we meet."

Next time being when? She wanted to say, but instead, her voice trembled as she said, "Looking forward to it." Nevaeh clutched tightly to her bag handles, her heart pounding in her chest. The words were there, but she couldn't say them. Not yet. She cleared her throat. "I'm just going to head out and tell everyone I know how much I just slayed," she grinned.

"You better. You did great tonight." Sean's hand reached out, stroking her cheek, lingering just a moment too long. "See you another time, okay Nevaeh?"

"Yes..." Nevaeh turned around, a fluttering heart and a desire she couldn't ignore. Five feet from Sean, the longing became too much. Without hesitation, she turned on her heel and sprinted towards him, their lips meeting in a fiery kiss that left them stunned.

It began as a small moment of affection, but then they were completely swept away by their passion. Sean's strong arms wrapped around her, pulling her closer, their mouths moving together in perfect rhythm. Time seemed to stop, the world falling away until there was only them.

They broke apart, and the air around them crackled with electricity. Nevaeh touched her lips, still tingling from his kiss. "Bye, Sean," she whispered, her eyes shining.

His signature cool smile followed her out the door, but his final words, "Bye, Nev," left her heart aching and soaring all at once.

As she passed Cynthia's desk, Nevaeh's bright smile confused the woman, but she felt like shouting from the rooftops. "Your boss is amazing!" she exclaimed, grabbing the ends of Cynthia's high desk. A satisfaction like no other settled her heart, a promise of something more, something deeper, just beginning to blossom.

The girl leaned back at the sudden exclamation, raising her hands off her keyboard. "Um… okay?" she laughed. "Someone had a good class, huh?"

"Yes!" Nevaeh left before screaming down the room. She wouldn't let Sean hear her uncontained enthusiasm.

In her car, Nevaeh instinctively whipped her phone out before driving. After opening her friends' group chat, she blinked at messages upon messages coming in. "Wait…" The further she read, the more her jaw dropped. "Shut up! Justin proposed!"

Courtney sent pictures of littered flower petals along the watch repair shop and a painting of her family heirloom watch, which brought her to Justin initially. The painting depicted the very hour Courtney's watch had broken, indicating the exact time destiny unfolded.

"Oh my God!" Nevaeh's heart flew higher. What a beautiful way to end a lovely dance practice. She sat taller and typed, sending infinite congrats to her girl Courtney. Things were looking up for all of them. Who knew? Maybe one day, Nevaeh would announce an epic proposal. She put her phone down and thought of Brandi's wedding. That brought thoughts of Matt. "He's already my date. No sense calling it off now."

Nevaeh revved her car engine and started on her way home. Courtney's proposal pictures came in an hour ago. She certainly wouldn't be at the watch shop right now, but Nevaeh might have swung by to freak out with her in person if she was.

She found a station playing old love songs. Sean's lips had left her fuzzy inside. She'd sleep happily tonight with Courtney's amazing news and Sean's greatness snuggling her tightly.

CHAPTER SEVENTEEN

Sean scribbled his signature on the designated line, tearing out the receipt with a flourish. "All right. Here you are, and thank you so much for signing up with 'Lights, Camera, Dance!' You're all set for your..." His voice trailed off, the correct terminology escaping him. He looked up at the group of moms before him, their lessons complete, their fees paid, confidence gained, but for what event he couldn't recall.

"We're doing a show at town square on Friday," one of the women announced, a white towel draped around her neck. Her friends admired Sean's accolades and certificates on the walls, four of them congregating around his college diploma. Sean's pride was tinged with impatience; his next student was due soon. Heaven herself. That's how he thought of Nevaeh, despite the corny feelings she stirred in him. "You should come watch us, Teach. See how well we learned," the woman added, leaning toward him suggestively.

"Sounds like fun. I'll see if I can make it," Sean replied, catching sight of his niece, Tia, dashing inside, an hour of hyperactivity behind her and the glow of summer all around. "T, want to go see some dancing on Friday?" he asked her. Tia, sparkling with her newly made friendship bracelet, agreed.

The first woman snapped her fingers. "That's the spirit," she folded Sean's receipt. "Can't wait to see you there," her friends left the wall to say goodbye, waving suggestively, chit-chatting as they left.

"Oh, by the way," one stopped before exiting. "That girl we always see coming in for lessons at this time,"

Sean packed the receipt book neatly with some folders he stored close by. "What about her?"

"I keep hearing that she's your girl. Is that true? Are you taken now, Mr. Martin?" the woman asked boldly. She dropped her voice, but it didn't change the question's nature. A few other ladies hung back, appearing to eavesdrop from the hall. Had they discussed this beforehand?

Sean was caught off guard by the bold question and his mouth went dry as he tried to formulate a response.

"Sean!" Suddenly, Nevaeh herself came barging into the room, classical music booming from her phone speaker. "Oh, wait, am I interrupting something?" Her hoodie looked damp in certain areas. "Sorry! I'll come back later."

"No, no, honey. Stay by all means. I was asking about classes and the like. Don't mind me. We were just leaving," the lady smartly puckered lips at Nevaeh while snickering. She gave Sean a knowing glance as she and her companions hurried off, obviously gossiping about what had happened.

Sean held his face in embarrassment. Was that what people thought? They weren't wrong, but he'd rather officially label things with Nevaeh before going public. Even though they got along well and enjoyed each other's time, he still didn't know where they'd end up because, as far as he knew, she still had her 'situationship' as she'd called it. *It doesn't matter, Sean.*

"Nevaeh, when did you get here?" He stood, brushing off those unwelcome thoughts. They still had ten minutes before class. Their second to last lesson before her friend's wedding.

Drawing in a breath, she said, "I rushed out of work early so I could get here and practice on my own before we began." She spun around excitedly, her eyes sparkling. "I know I'm not perfect, but I did it again with no mistakes. I truly believe I'm ready to amaze Brandi. What's your opinion? But wait, look... Tia, come here and be my partner," she continued, her hands playfully reaching out to beckon the seven-year-old.

"Okey-doke," Tia skipped to Nevaeh and took her hands. "Nevaeh, I have to tell you all about what me and Jamilia did today."

"Ladies, I believe we should move this to the practice room. That way, you'll have enough space," Sean said, his heart pounding with anticipation for the upcoming lesson.

The previous weekend without her had been lackluster and uneventful. Sean and Neveah had unexpectedly run into each other at the supermarket but failed to make dinner plans. Since Tia hadn't been with him, the child couldn't play matchmaker. Sean could tell from their lingering gazes that they both wanted to spend more time together after their shopping. Nevaeh had been giving Sean all the signals, but he still didn't make a move. Fear and insecurity had kept him at bay.

In two weeks, another man would be Nevaeh's companion to her friend's wedding. That thought had been enough for Sean to resist temptation at that moment, but now regret gnawed at his heart, beating with longing for her. Could he make up for the lost opportunity now, even with that Matt person still in the picture? Was Sean getting in too deep when Nevaeh hadn't given him any indication that she wanted to upgrade their relationship and kick Matt to the curb?

"Good idea. This office isn't wide enough, and I'd *hate* to spin into the wall by accident," Nevaeh said, bringing Sean back to the moment. She swung her hand in Tia's. "Tell me all about Jamilia's house—" a modern song with disco production suddenly replaced Nevaeh's classical Waltz piece. She jumped at the shift looking startled.

"Nevaeh, isn't that your ringtone?" Sean asked. He'd heard that tune a few times already.

"Yeah," she laughed awkwardly and whipped out her cell. "Oops. Sorry, guys," she said as she ran out of the room to answer it. "Hello?"

Tia peeped out the door. "I wonder who she's talking to."

Sean heard noises of disagreement. From his view, Nevaeh looked enraged. She paced the hall angrily with a fixed frown, calling whoever she spoke to 'unreliable' and 'a waste of time.'

"We should probably mind our own business," Sean said as he gently tugged Tia away from the door. "If you want, you can tell me more about Jamilia's house and your doll game."

"You're speaking my language, Uncle Sean," Tia clicked her tongue, then got down to business.

Ten minutes later, Nevaeh returned, visibly upset.

"Everything okay?" Sean asked as she shoved her phone into her pocket with a sigh of frustration. Nevaeh pressed her temples, eyes closed, her brows betraying her inner turmoil. It was clear something on that phone call had upset her, and Sean worried about how it might affect their lesson. "Come on, take a seat, Nev."

Sean pulled out a chair and gestured for Nevaeh to sit down, which she did, clearly perturbed.

Nevaeh clenched her fists, but kept them in her lap. "I'm so disappointed," she said with measured anger. "I knew this was a long time coming, but I kept putting it off."

Sean caught Tia's eye and motioned for her to give him and Nevaeh some privacy to talk. Tia nodded and silently left the room, closing the door behind her.

Nevaeh's eyes, usually so bright, were shadowed with irritation. But there was more sadness than rage in them. "He had one job! And the only reason I didn't end things was because we agreed to go as dates to Brandi's wedding, but now he's saying he won't be in town?" She shook her head, more in sorrow than in anger. "He needs to learn to prioritize his commitments. It's not like he's a child. It's just so irresponsible."

"Hey, hey, hey," Sean said, squatting in front of her. "I understand why you're upset, and you have every right to be. But don't let this guy ruin your day or your lesson with me." He took her hand, concern in his eyes. "We'll figure something out for the wedding."

Nevaeh looked at Sean, her swelling emotions apparent. "You're right. I just can't believe—no, I can believe he would do this, but it doesn't make it any less frustrating. What am I going to do now?"

"So is your relationship with Matt over?" Sean asked.

"I mean, it wasn't much of a relationship, but we're definitely off permanently. I just made that quite clear to him," Nevaeh said, meeting Sean's eyes.

Sean sensed an opportunity and took a gentle breath, preparing himself. "Nevaeh, I know this might sound sudden, especially after everything that's happened with Matt, but would you consider going to the wedding with me?"

Nevaeh's eyes widened, and for a moment, she looked lost for words. Sean continued, "I mean, we've spent time together, and I know I'm not a replacement for what you had planned, but I would be honored to accompany you. I promise to do my best to make it a memorable experience."

Nevaeh sniffed audibly after gasping. He hadn't seen when tears spilled out, but they dampened the area around her puffy eyes. "Sean, really? You would do that for me?"

"Of course," Sean reassured her, squeezing her hands. "You deserve to have a wonderful time at the wedding, and I would love to be the one to share it with you."

Her face broke into a grateful smile, and she clutched Sean's hands tightly in her lap. "Thank you, Sean. You're amazing. You've just lifted a weight off my shoulders."

His face rested upon her shoulder, where Sean felt her heartbeat. Though rapid, the rhythm tamed his inner restlessness, melting away that deep-rooted fear that they'd never evolve because of Matt's involvement. Sean breathed out with closing eyes and embraced her. "No Nevaeh. Thank you."

CHAPTER EIGHTEEN

With the thrilling thought that Sean was now her date to the wedding, Nevaeh looked both ways, her mind ablaze with excitement. The summer heat bore down relentlessly, and she sheltered herself under an umbrella, just as others did, protecting against the midday sun's wrath. On this bustling Friday, the streets were lively, filled with fellow pedestrians stalking the sidewalk, umbrellas raised like shields against UV rays. Nevaeh felt a part of the action and welcomed it, especially since she had a special lunch date that day—one more intimate than her usual meetups with friends like Brandi.

Quickening her pace, she reached Main Street and headed past familiar landmarks: Mrs. Zhang's restaurant, the tax office, and Joanne's coffee place. After a brief pause for breath, she regarded the building before her, contemplating how full the street was with parked cars. "How many students does he see at working hours?" she wondered aloud, glad she'd decided to walk rather than wrestle with parking.

Before entering, Nevaeh checked her appearance in her phone camera, satisfied with what she saw. She kissed the screen affection-ately, placing it back in her handbag, which complemented her stylish black, cuffed, polka-dotted blouse and dark dress pants. Despite some teasing from co-workers for her meticulous attention to makeup, she knew that everything about this meeting had to be perfect.

Pushing open the hot glass doors, she greeted Cynthia at the front desk.

"I don't have you down for lessons right now," Cynthia said, momentarily pausing her salad lunch and spreadsheet work. The lobby, devoid of music and visitors, looked strangely quiet.

Nevaeh, who had always appreciated Cynthia's directness, smiled and replied, "That's because I'm not here for that." Her handbag slid to her elbow as she glanced around the hall. "Sean's here, right?" Memories of her conversation with Matt flitted through her mind, followed by a more pleasant recollection of Sean's rescue. She had spent hours pondering her feelings, her relationships, and how Sean's qualities outshone all others. That night, as she lay in bed, the realization had struck her with clarity, prompting her to arrange this date. Sean's enthusiastic acceptance had filled her with joy, setting the stage for this new chapter in their relationship. A chapter where Nevaeh was fully comfortable exploring Sean as a partner, with Matt officially in the past.

Sean appeared from down the corridor, arms spread wide in an inviting embrace, and a captivating cologne filled the air around Nevaeh like a fresh spring breeze. "Wow. That work outfit sure is cute," he said as he hugged her and planted a kiss on her left cheek. "I don't think I've ever seen you dressed up for your nine-to-five."

His twinkling eyes and radiant grin sent a wave of warmth through Nevaeh, affirming her decision to meet him. "Thanks, Sean. I actually don't wear this often," she admitted, intertwining her hand with his.

His left brow arched mischievously, and a playful smirk danced on his face. "Is it safe to assume you wore this for me?" he teased, squinting as they stepped into the sun.

Nevaeh opened her umbrella, shielding them from the fierce

sunlight. Sean took it from her and held it over them as she searched for her sunglasses. "And you could say I wore something special just for you, or you could say I wore it for me to feel confident. Whichever works best," she said, sliding on her shades with an air of self-assurance.

"I like the confident option better, so I'll go with it," Sean chuckled, expertly twirling her scarlet umbrella, their arms bound together as naturally as magnets.

They wandered toward Mrs Zhang's restaurant, Sweet and Spicy Chinese Palace, a favorite local spot for Chinese cuisine. Nevaeh wondered if it might be too soon to label what she and Sean had, but she couldn't ignore the spark between them. She felt as though they were already a couple, and she wanted to see where this connection would lead.

As they approached the bustling restaurant, Nevaeh excitedly pointed out the spicy ramen on the standup sign. "Ooo, you have got to try it, Sean!" she exclaimed, clutching his hand. "Oh crud. If we stay outside too long, we won't get seats!" she urged, pulling him inside.

The cool air-conditioning greeted them as they entered the packed space, filled with the delicious aroma of noodles, spicy sauce, and sushi. After a brief hunt, Nevaeh spotted a corner table by the bathroom adorned with a golden dragon—a symbol of the restaurant's theme.

"It's okay with me," Sean agreed, strolling with her between the occupied tables. They paused briefly at the counter, uncertain whether to order or claim their seats.

Nevaeh came to a sudden realization. "Yes! Let's order first. The line's not too long, so we won't lose our place."

They soon settled contentedly into their corner booth, eagerly anticipating their meal.

Nevaeh favored Chow Mein, and she didn't dare attempt eating with chopsticks, attacking her meal instead with a fork. "Never eaten here before?" she asked Sean, who was eating generous portions of noodles.

They sat face to face, and Sean wiped his mouth with his napkin. "Quite a few times, actually," he said, sipping his tea. "It's close to the studio, so it's convenient for lunch." His glance flicked to his own chopsticks. "You seem like a big fan of this restaurant."

Nevaeh twirled noodles around her fork. "Oh yes. The owner's a friend of mine. We go to the book club together at Rochelle's Old Fashioned Diner. She's really nice."

Sean began to fiddle with his chopsticks. "I agree. The few times she and I conversed, I thought she was really cool."

"Yep," Nevaeh said, mesmerized by his handling of the utensils. "You know how to use those?" she asked.

"No, but it feels wrong sitting in a Chinese restaurant eating with forks," Sean said, finally getting the hang of the chopsticks. "Now I'm in business. So, the wedding's in the church garden, right?"

Nevaeh felt upstaged by his newfound skill with the chopsticks. "In the garden outside," she replied, her thoughts drifting. "We thought an outdoor wedding might be more beautiful. And thank you again for being my date. Maybe I'd have hired an escort to take with me if you hadn't said yes."

He laughed. "You're funny. It's no problem. It was kind of a no-brainer that I would take you, right?"

"Yes," she affirmed. "After all, you and I have something special. We went out, had dinner, I met your parents, and spent a lot of time together..." His eyes brightened. "The only thing missing is—"

"To seal the deal?" Sean teased. "Call you mine while I stamp 'Nevaeh's Property' on my cheek?"

Her heart fluttered. "Aww. You wouldn't have to do that, though I'm not saying you shouldn't." She giggled. "But seriously, let's make us a thing. A relationship between you and me. Sean and Nevaeh. What do you say?"

"I've been on board with that idea since I saw you," Sean said, his words making her swoon. "So that's that? We already did everything couples do, right?"

"That's how it happens sometimes, baby. Think there's something wrong with that?"

"Not at all," he said, clacking the chopsticks. "As long as we're end game, I'm here for the Nevaeh ride."

"How do you do that?" she finally asked, attempting to use her chopsticks. Sean patiently taught her, and in minutes, she used them proficiently, screeching delightedly.

"You did amazing." Sean smiled at her enthusiasm. "As much as I've enjoyed our time, we're past our lunch break. We're late."

Nevaeh lost track of time. "Oh, no! Let's go. Call me later?"

Sean pulled her in for a forehead kiss. "My pleasure. Let me walk you back to work," he said, taking her hand. They left, fingers intertwined, heads close, both content with their status as a couple.

CHAPTER NINETEEN

"I would have had it there, but it's too far. Brands would suspect something if one of us drove her out of town," Nevaeh chatted enthusiastically at the dinner table that evening. Surrounding speakers filled the room with Brandi's favorite songs, thanks to 'Dine and Party's' DJ. Pink lights illuminated the area, matching the color theme Nevaeh had chosen for the night. Their table was centrally positioned, with a perfect view of the stage, while other tables were stacked to the side.

"I would have figured it out anyway. You guys wouldn't let me get married without throwing a bachelorette party. You're the best friends a girl could ask for," Brandi said, adjusting her gold crown. The girls had surprised her after work, and they'd spent the evening enjoying good music and wine, all according to Nevaeh's meticulous planning.

They all agreed, giggling merrily, clearly enjoying the wine. The waitstaff, wearing pink T-shirts arranged by Nevaeh, began to clean up behind the bar. Nevaeh had been the driving force behind the night, aiming for perfection, and she'd achieved it. Brandi never looked happier, and the girls were already looking forward to a sleepover at Courtney's later.

"Of course, we wouldn't let you go without one, especially since you mentioned wanting a party," Nevaeh refilled her glass, encouraging Brandi to let loose. "I even arranged karaoke since I know you like it."

The girls laughed and babbled, chaos ensuing as usual when they were together. They discussed plans for singing, with Courtney suggesting breakup songs, although her suggestion was met with raised eyebrows. They reminisced about their childhood, singing along to cheesy boybands long since forgotten.

Nevaeh tried to cut Courtney off from the wine, but Brandi insisted they all go wild, nearly spilling the drink in the process. They all laughed at the antics, glad Nevaeh had rented out the whole place. Courtney insisted on singing a particular song, although she struggled to describe it properly.

"I know the song you're talking about, but you didn't describe it right," Nevaeh said, sliding out of the booth and stumbling to the floor.

Her friends laughed as she landed, knowing that they could always find humor in each other's mishaps. They'd always have each other's back, and the comfort of that support was priceless.

Minutes later, Nevaeh took the stage, whispering Courtney's song to the DJ. As the instrumental began, the girls recognized an old hit from their teen years.

"Come on up, girls. Let's sing some tunes together," Nevaeh called, dancing freely. She was handed a mic and embraced her inner star as the others joined her on stage, with Courtney scrambling up in her excitement.

"Oh boy, Court, I hope you don't fall over while we sing," Nevaeh chuckled, helping her friend find her balance.

In no time at all, they were all up on stage, mics in hand, voices belting out the tune. Joanne had the best voice of the group, though she'd never pursued singing seriously. In stark contrast, Nevaeh and Brandi croaked like wounded frogs, their off-key notes only adding to the fun. Courtney, overcome with laughter, howled more than she sang, her joyous noise capturing the essence of their wonderful time together.

LATER THAT EVENING at Courtney's place, they spread their sleeping bags across the living room floor, each one filled with anticipation for a night of fun. Joanne, Courtney, and Nevaeh had bought an assortment of junk food after work, and with Saturday looming, they had the entire night to indulge. Singing at karaoke had already lifted their spirits, making them eager for more entertainment. Justin, at Nevaeh's request, arranged to stay at a friend's house, leaving the girls alone. Nevaeh preferred it this way, doubting Justin would sleep if he had stayed.

Nevaeh smiled at the sound of crumpling plastic and crunching food. Crossing her legs on her sleeping bag, she gripped her socked ankles as their bags formed a ring where the couch used to be, now pushed aside for more room. "I don't know which one to choose!" she exclaimed, slapping her cheeks. Brandi and Courtney's engagement rings were the topic of much admiration, both women showing them off with pride and complimenting each other endlessly.

"And you won't have to because neither of them are yours," Joanne teased, dusting crumbs into her chip bag. She pinched Nevaeh's cheek, causing her to yelp. They all wore bonnets, large T-shirts, and cozy bottoms, the unofficial uniform of their group. Though Nevaeh hadn't tied up her hair, she planned to soon in case she unintentionally fell asleep. Midnight had just passed, and one a.m. was fast approaching. Time certainly did fly when friends united.

"Ow!" Nevaeh protested, snatching Joanne's bag and helping herself to some chips. "Who would have thought that two out of four of us would end up engaged before thirty?"

"I would have never imagined it, but I guess anything is possible," Courtney replied, clapping and shimmying forward. She hugged a pillow to her chest, wearing one of Justin's oversized T-shirts. "I just can't wait for Brandi's wedding. She's going to look absolutely stunning!"

As the girls continued to chat, Brandi shyly admitted her excitement, Joanne expressed her disdain for Nevaeh's ex, and Nevaeh cleverly turned the tables on Joanne's relationship advice. A playful argument broke out, leading to Nevaeh's mischievous pillow attack.

Joanne responded by throwing the pillow and tackling Nevaeh, spilling chips everywhere. Courtney, filled with the lively spirit from the bar, chugged her soda and scolded them, "Don't make a mess. Trust you two to do something stupid." Brandi, entertained by the silly exchange, made it clear she wasn't helping clean up.

Amidst the laughter, wriggling, and tickling, Nevaeh's thoughts turned to Sean, Tia, and the unexpected turn her love life had taken. A teenage Nevaeh would have never believed she'd fall for a single dad. Yet, here she was, in love with both Sean and his bundle of joy. *Love?* she thought. *Yes, I do love him.* She held that thought tight until sleep overcame her.

CHAPTER TWENTY

Sean had never escorted Nevaeh to her car before, but it seemed fitting given what today marked: the last class. Though he'd been dreading this day, he knew it would come. Nevaeh couldn't stay a student forever.

Standing by her car, Nevaeh folded her lips and clung tightly to her bag. "So… I guess this is it until Saturday?" she asked, popping her door handle open.

Sean gave room on the sidewalk for the door to swing open, his back to the studio. "Yeah. Unless we text tonight," he replied, a longing in his voice.

"Oh yeah! Texting. How could I forget that option?" Nevaeh teased. Her eyes lost focus as she grew quiet. "So, text tonight?"

"I'll be sure to do that," Sean said, not wanting her to go. After complimenting her on her progress, she shut her car door cheerfully, turning back to him.

"Oh, Sean, stop doing that," she laughed. "You practically threw me a party in the practice room after I danced just now," she mimed some steps, "But if you want, you can continue. I don't mind. I like how you praise me."

Sean couldn't help but love that side of her. "No, really. Your determination was everything. I don't think I've ever met anyone so hellbent on learning... I can't wait to watch you kill that waltz on Saturday. You'll be the life of the party for a different reason," he said, drawing closer, taking her by the hand.

Nevaeh looked flattered as he raised her hand to his lips and kissed her fingers. "Thank you, Sean. I wouldn't have accomplished any of it without you... Everything I've accomplished is because of you. So, thank you."

Sean refused to take all the credit. "You did a lot of this on your own, though... Are we doing one last dance to call it a day?"

"I just like showing off, even if there's no one here," Nevaeh admitted with a snigger. They commenced a merry waltz, capering freely, eventually locking eyes as if their lives depended on it.

When they stopped together, Sean pulled her close, staring head on. Nevaeh did the same, and they shared a passionate kiss. The kiss began to escalate, and Sean pulled back.

"What?" she asked breathlessly.

Sean, panting, replied, "We don't want a court case on our hands, do we?"

Nevaeh laughed, hiding her face against Sean's chest. "Why didn't you stop me sooner, you accomplice!" she joked.

"How could I when I'd been having the time of my life?" Sean teased back, but his next words surprised her: "Is it expected for someone to willingly interrupt the love of their life?"

"Love of your life?" Nevaeh asked, her eyes wide.

"Yes. The love of my life," Sean confirmed, a warmth in his voice.

"It did happen fast, didn't it?" she said shyly.

"But I heard that the greatest loves usually do," he answered. "Am I crazy for confessing?"

"No!" she cried. "I might have confessed the same thing to myself already... So, if you're crazy, then I am too. But you knew that," she said, pulling a playful face.

Sean laughed at her humor. "I love you, Nevaeh," he replied, brushing her cheek. "I do. And I can't wait to dance with you on Saturday after you finish your waltz..."

Nevaeh embraced Sean with a sudden burst of affection. "I love you too, Sean! You and Tia... I don't know what I'd do if I hadn't met you. You're so incredible and kind and amazing. I want us to be together for a long time to come. Even if we fell in love out of nowhere," she rambled on.

Sean caught every word and held her between his arms. As she drove off later, he watched, already missing the connection of her skin.

CHAPTER TWENTY-ONE

Brandi's outdoor wedding on a bright, sunny day was a stunning sight to behold. It was the perfect day - the sun was shining, and there wasn't a cloud in the sky. Nevaeh had been worried about the heat, but the clear skies and occasional breeze made for a comfortable day.

Brandi's chosen location and time—around eight a.m. in the church's back garden—definitely aided in warding off discomfort. The scene looked magical as the morning glow added an ethereal touch before the sun's wrath would begin after eleven. The stunning white rose wreaths were tied with ribbons to every chair, and hand-made flowery arches dotted the aisle and altar.

Upon arrival, guests were each given a silver dove-themed pin to wear for the duration of the event. Flower girls tossed white petals along the silver aisle to the melody of "Here Comes the Bride."

The bridal party walked forward in crepe dresses of varying designs but all the same shade. Chris's groomsmen wore gray suits, while he himself chose a black tuxedo. Brandi's gown was reminiscent of old fairy tales she loved—wide-skirted, flowing at the end, and off-the-shoulder. Her hair twisted in a braid adorned with jaw-dropping white lilies and shiny pearls.

As Chris laid eyes on her, he aptly said, "My love, you stand as heaven's pride before me," and tears welled in many eyes. She truly shone like a gem from above.

The ceremony culminated in joyful cheers as Brandi kissed Chris, who then carried her down the aisle to lively pop tunes. The special ice doves on the back table drew gasps from the crowd, and Nevaeh's heart swelled with pride for her friend Brandi. The wedding was a resounding success, and she patted herself on the back for having helped. But what churned her stomach was how her dance at the reception would go. Soon, at the convention hall that afternoon, she would find out.

The hall was tastefully decorated with tables and chairs arranged along its perimeter, creating a spacious central area. The spherical disco ball hanging from the ceiling illuminated the entire room with its colorful light. The tables were immaculate, with white cloths that flowed down to the floor and dove-shaped centerpieces.

Nevaeh stood outside the decorated doorway, inhaling deep breaths, her nerves mounting. Her feet crunched on gravel as she paced in her ill-suited heels. "Oh my God, what if I trip on our way in, guys?" she whispered.

"You're not going to trip," Joanne assured her, squeezing her friend's rib. "Didn't you see yourself last night? You danced like a pro, Nev. Give yourself some credit."

Soon enough, the organizer, a slender, kind, yet firm woman, called them to order. Her sharp attention to detail had added the finishing touches to the event, and she now demanded perfection.

"No," whispered Nevaeh, standing beside Gabriel, her waltz partner, and wishing Sean was her dance partner instead. Unfortunately, the bridal party had to do the official dance with the groomsmen.

Their entrance was magical, filled with anticipation and grace. As they filed in to dulcet violins, phone lights twinkled like stars, and Nevaeh's eyes darted through the assembled crowd.

Her heart was pounding, and her focus was pulled away from

the dance as she searched for one face among the many. Then, she found him—Sean, her source of comfort and encouragement. Their eyes locked, and he smiled reassuringly, mouthing the words, "You got this."

In that moment, the room seemed to fade away, and all her fears dissolved. His presence, that simple gesture, was all she needed to glide through the dance with confidence and grace.

As the waltz unfolded, Nevaeh stepped cleanly, switching places with her friends and adding spice to their dance. Finally, they made way for Chris and Brandi, whose entrance was met with resounding applause.

"Awesome job," said Gabriel after they finished, joining the crowd.

"Don't you want to capture this?" Courtney, tears in her eyes, pinched Nevaeh's arm, recording the moment.

Nevaeh snapped out of her stupor, tears of relief in her eyes. "I think you've got me covered in terms of recording," she replied, realizing all her hard work had paid off.

At last, she could relax and enjoy the reception, admiring how heavenly Brandi looked, her eyes still damp with joy.

⁂

After delivering a heartfelt speech as Brandi's maid of honor, Nevaeh found her place beside Sean, who had retreated from the dancing and games. Evening had set in, and the reception was in full swing. DJ Groovy was working magic on the crowd, and the infectious vibes were undeniable. Still, Nevaeh's heart ached a little to step aside.

"Mr. Dancing-man prefers eating in a corner instead of partying?" she teased, taking her seat. They had danced and celebrated earlier, but now Sean looked worn out.

Sean grinned, running a napkin over his lips. "Right now, yes. I'm building back my strength. But why aren't you out there? You were rocking that dance solo earlier," he said with that easy smile she loved.

Nevaeh playfully cringed at the memory. "Don't remind me! I bet I looked silly."

Sean's face softened. "No way. You were having fun. I loved watching you," he assured her, then turned serious. "Your waltz was perfect, by the way."

She felt a flutter in her stomach. "You might have mentioned that," she said, then her tone turned sincere. "And thank you, Sean. Brandi said it reminded her of Cinderella. It went perfectly because of you. I truly am grateful."

"I know, Nevaeh, I know," Sean said, relaxing back in his chair. "Your friends sure know how to party. Just look at Justin trying to dance with Courtney!"

They both laughed at the sight. "That's adorable, but hilarious," Nevaeh agreed.

"I like it, though. He's trying for her," Sean said, chuckling.

"The mood here is everything. You're not a big partier, are you?" Nevaeh nudged him teasingly.

Sean shrugged. "I did my share of dancing earlier. Gotta eat to keep up my strength for the last dance. You and I should take center stage, just like during that hip hop track," he laughed as he playfully imitated some dance moves Nevaeh had done to the song he referenced.

"You scoundrel!" Nevaeh laughed, hiding her face in his shoulder. "Today was great, so why not? You and me, ultimate duo. What do you say?"

"Any time, any day. Just call me," Sean agreed, high-fiving her.

Nevaeh's eyes sparkled. "If you fall, I'll carry you to the sidelines. Don't worry, baby," she said, grabbing his hand and leading him back to the dance floor.

EPILOGUE

9:00 *p.m.*The wedding reception for Brandi and Chris was drawing to a close, a record-breaker for sure. As Sean leaned against a wide square window with Nevaeh nestled into his chest, their eyes fixed on the stars outside, he knew his little Tia would be sound asleep at his parents' house.

Though the newlyweds had already departed and all guests had left, Sean stuck around with Nevaeh, leaning near a wide square window. Together, they looked above the outside wall as stars lit the night with their twinkling radiance.

"I hope we're not getting in the way," Nevaeh murmured, her voice soft and content. "We're the only guests here. They're packing up the tables. If Tia's at your parents' place, I could spend the night. Would that be okay?"

Sean's heart warmed at the thought. He kissed her nose and replied, "It would, but there's something I want to do first."

He fished for his phone, the clamping and clanging of the staff folding tables and packing dishes creating a rhythmic backdrop to their intimate moment. DJ Groovy and his assistants were winding cables on stage, preparing to pack away.

"Really?" Nevaeh peeked at Sean's screen, her curiosity piqued.

"Hold on," Sean hid it by giving her his back. He found what he wanted then rested the phone in the window. The design made it large enough to sit in. In fact, he'd caught people doing so; when they could party no more and were too stuffed to dance.

"Oh! We're having one last dance before we go?" Nevaeh's eyes twinkled. "Let's do it! They moved all the chairs so now we have lots of room."

She hauled him to the dance floor before he could move. Sean laughed then spun her like a top. After doing so, he held her against him. They shared another kiss in which he savored every second, shutting his eyes while their foreheads met. He found solace in her familiar embrace, with her arms on his shoulders and his hands on her waist.

Nevaeh's beauty knew no bounds and touched him in ways mere words were simply incapable of describing. If only love truly had its own language. Where, by cherishing someone, their perspective of how they are seen can be better understood. He had fallen for heaven herself, and no amount of gestures or proclamations could capture the intensity of his feelings.

Not a soul looked away as they grooved to his playlist. Sean thought they'd be asked to leave, but staff members gladly watched. *Good,* in hind sight, he should have provided a warning. Just so they'd know, he'd stay back. How grateful he was for their cooperation.

When the music faded as his last song closed off, Nevaeh clapped high and thanked him for the dance. "Aww, Sean. That was just so, *so* romantic. Though I wish we'd gotten to— Sean?" she leaned her head to the side as Sean backed up. "What are you doing?"

Sean began waltzing to no music, taking on a princely aura. She stared at him oddly, trying to figure out what was happening. He dropped the act to grin with a hand in his back pocket, saying nothing to her questions.

Nevaeh held her hand out, expecting him to take it now that

they met face to face again, but instead, Sean dropped to one knee, a small box in hand.

The room erupted in cheers, the staff's joy filling the room. DJ Groovy's enthusiastic shout of "You go, boy!" echoed through the hall.

Nevaeh's face registered pure shock, tears in her eyes. "Sean," she whispered.

Sean loved her even more for responding so profoundly. He saw phone lights shining as others ran to look. Gushing and giggling rose to his ears. Try as he might to get her alone tonight; nothing worked out. He didn't mind the small crowd, but had planned for this to be intimate. *It works either way.* Because to him, she alone counted as present in the room.

"Nevaeh Carr, I can't imagine life without you. I've said it all a million times, how much you mean to me and how deeply I feel for you. You know. You know just how perfectly you complete me, so I won't waste any time and just get to the point. Will you make me the happiest person to ever walk this earth and marry me?"

Five women with dishes were fawning by the door, and the excitement in the room was palpable.

"Yes! Of course, Sean! I can't believe you got me so good!" Nevaeh cried, her joy uncontainable. "I had no idea, Sean! You caught me! Yes! Yes, I'll marry you. I'll marry you in every life time! I love you so much!"

Her response left Sean breathless, his grin so wide it hurt. He slid the heart-shaped diamond ring onto her finger, whispering, "Perfect."

Sean let her pepper kisses all over his face. "I really wanted to surprise you."

Destiny brought them together, and soon they'd be married. Tia might burst open when given the news. Only Justin was aware of his plan.

Their kiss sealed their promise, a promise of forever. Sean knew he'd found paradise in Nevaeh, a love that would last a lifetime. The night had been long, but it ended with the beginning of their forever. They looked out at the twinkling stars, knowing that their love story was just as eternal, just as bright, with the echoes of the staff's cheers still lingering in the air, adding to the magic of the moment.

AUTHOR'S NOTE

Thank you so much for reading Dance With Me, the fourth book in the Sweetgum Meadows Romance series of stand-alone novels. I really hope you loved it! If you enjoyed this book, please consider leaving it a review so that others may also find it. Also, if you haven't read the first three books, yet, check them out today! Although these are stand-alone novels, the stories all intertwine and progress.

I look forward to introducing you to the other characters in this lovely, family-oriented town where each couple will find their happily ever after.

Would you like to receive bonus scenes and keep up with what's next with my upcoming books? Then, make sure you sign up for my mailing list on my website by visiting ImaniPrice.com.

ALSO BY IMANI PRICE

Book 1: Love Between Us

Book 2: Sweet Sunsets

Book 3: Infinite Kiss

Book 4: Dance With Me

Book 5: In Charge

Book 6: Forever With You

Book 7: Secret Sweethearts

Book 8: Endless Love

Book 9: The Harder We Fall

Book 10: Reservations of the Heart

Book 11: Play by Play

Book 12: Guarded Hearts

Book 13: Healing Hearts

Book 14: Dear Sweetgum

Book 15: Lanterns of the Meadows (novella)

Book 16: Drawn to You

Book 17: Under the Sweetgum Tree

Sweetgum Meadows' Visitor's Guide

My full audiobook catalog is available for FREE on YouTube. Check it out here: https://swiy.co/Sweetgum

To all my lovely readers,

Thank you for reading